Miss Barbellion's Garden

MISS BARBELLION'S GARDEN

🌿 🌿 🌿 🌿

written by
Irving Finkel
and
illustrated by
Jenny Kallin

K&B
Kennedy & Boyd

Kennedy & Boyd
an imprint of
Zeticula Ltd
The Roan,
Kilkerran,
KA19 8LS,
Scotland

http://www.kennedyandboyd.co.uk
admin@kennedyandboyd.co.uk

Text Copyright © Irving Finkel 2012
Illustrations Copyright © Jenny Kallin 2012

ISBN 978 1 84921 071 3

This book is dedicated to
Jemima B.
and
Julia C.
and
Sophie R.
and
Phoebe J.

ABOUT MISS BARBELLION

When the solicitor's letter reached her in India in July 1987 to say that she had inherited the house in Bath in accordance with her father's will, Miss Barbellion decided there and then to go home and live in it herself. The timing was perfect. She was seventy-one years old and had been wondering for more than a year about her long-term future. She had been away from England and her birthplace of Bath for forty-eight years, and a huge leap would therefore be required, even though 1987 was not, in fact, a leap year.

Nancy Rochester Barbellion was the last survivor of seven children, and while she had never been married, her life had been full of adventures in many parts of the world. Her father, the Reverend Edward Chauncey Barbellion, had successfully courted her mother Alva Philomel by the year 1892. The first daughter of Nancy's oldest sister, Belinda Ann, had already reached the age of eleven months by the time that Nancy herself was born, in 1916, on the very noteworthy date of *February 29th*. Miss Barbellion had accordingly been an *aunt* from her very first moment.

Admission to Cambridge to read for a degree in Theology had earned her a gilded entry on one of the painted mahogany boards in the school hall, although the decision greatly dismayed her headmistress, for Nancy was formidably able in Mathematics and Chemistry, and she had long been nourishing secret hopes for her pupil. Nancy's father, however, was delighted to support her in her choice; none of her siblings had ever responded much to his profession beyond obedient and more or less regular attendance at church. At university Nancy studied and read widely. One interesting young theologian in Cambridge turned out to have a carefully constructed and quite misleading public image, but there were no long-term consequences to prevent her from distinguishing herself admirably in her final examinations.

Miss Barbellion then found herself facing the question of what she should do with her life. The Reverend Barbellion proffered one short piece of much-considered advice: *always to help other people as much and as often as possible.* After a lifetime of fulfilling clerical responsibilities he had come to the conclusion that this dictum was the one important thing, and more or less implied (although he didn't actually admit it) that the rest was frippery. As it turned out, this word in her ear was sufficient for Miss Barbellion to find her feet. A chance contact led her to apply for a post in an understaffed mission school in China, and, before she knew where she was, the coast of England was receding behind her, and she was struggling with the help of a second-hand Jesuit grammar to master the essentials of Mandarin.

This posting proved to be but the beginning of a lifetime's work in places where managing births and injections or teaching reading and writing counted quite as much as bible classes and other more formal Mission activities. Life in strenuous circumstances and inhospitable climates brought out seemingly endless strength in Miss Barbellion. She found she was good at picking up unfamiliar languages so that nervous mothers or sceptical fathers would always know they could trust her. She loved other religions and was often to be found asking people questions about what they believed which they had never asked themselves. Mission work took her in turn to India, Burma and Ceylon, and by the time she was supposed to be thinking of retirement she was back in India, up on the North-Eastern frontier, teaching wide-eyed children their own and English letters (and how to help others).

Miss Barbellion had been taught by her mother always to answer letters immediately and she invariably did so. She was always fully up-to-date with her family's complicated lives and new children and maintained a burgeoning family tree, drawn in ink on a large and much-folded sheet of hand-made Indian paper, kept in her knitting bag. She had also the widest correspondence round the world, for former colleagues always wrote to her for news.

During the Second World War her work in the East had involved many remarkable episodes. After the death of her father in 1948, she spent a discreet fortnight in an English country house learning things that had never been mentioned at University. Later, close-written Barbellion letters would be addressed from some distant hill country or troubled border to an obscure room in Whitehall, although this side of her correspondence never led to a reply.

There were two particularly important Barbellion letter writers. One was Cynthia Margery Dimmock, whom she had known since the first day of primary school and who, over the decades, had run antique businesses and husbands in a variety of English cities; the Cynthia section in Miss Barbellion's disintegrating address book was full of crossings-out. The second was Elizabeth Dean, with whom she had shared digs at university. The two of them had steadfastly remained in contact ever since. Elizabeth was a writer; that is, she had certainly published books, which Miss Barbellion always read right through although without great enjoyment, but Elizabeth, too, was a cherished correspondent.

The head of the outwardly elderly lady who once again came to climb the steps of her old-and-new house was, therefore, stuffed with unusual experiences and dramatic memories, but her movements were quick and light as she turned the key in the lock, and the excitement that lit up her heart was like that of a young girl on the brink of adventure who had never even been away...

to climb the steps

1.

The house in Bath was as tall and narrow as ever, and Miss Barbellion remembered her mother complaining a thousand times about all the stairs, and wondered whether she herself was now going to end up uttering the same lament. The odd joint gave her a twinge now and again, but she could still run for the bus and still remember the Kings and Queens of England in order. Her own girlhood bedroom had been at the back on the second floor; there were two further floors above, the highest of all being the children's playroom, which ran the length and width of the house. The trouble now was that all the good furniture that Miss Barbellion remembered so well seemed to have ended up in the playroom, piled up and impenetrable. Even her father's desk was there, together with inherited stuff that she could remember her mother polishing, or wanting to keep away from boys with penknives.

She knew that her last sister, Leila Jane, who had been living in the house for the previous twenty years or so with her husband, had taken in lodgers at various times. There were two run-down kitchens upstairs and several gloomy bathrooms, but with a bit of attention and paint they could all be made a good deal more hospitable. Miss Barbellion wanted friends and acquaintances to come and stay, and the layout of the house as it now was would conveniently allow generous privacy for hostess and guests. Several young drama students in the house over the road seemed to have ample time on their hands and proved enthusiastic movers and decorators in return for staunch meals and spending money. By early October, three months after the solicitor had handed over the bunch of keys that had once belonged to her father, Miss Barbellion had got things more or less organised. She had made a new bedroom for herself on the first floor in what had once been her parents' bedroom. Her father's desk was now downstairs in the sitting room, with four of his old bookcases and many of his old books. It was a long time since she had read any theology and she was looking forward to a bit of a refresher course. After a few more weeks her long-suffering trunks arrived from India and she was glad to have her own familiar bits and pieces with her again.

The old family piano had always wobbled alarmingly but now it also sounded dreadful. Miss Barbellion found a local, old-school piano-tuner, who was soon muttering over the innards, and mentioning that he knew a good varnisher and a proper, strict piano teacher. It was a good fifty-five years since Miss Barbellion had last had a piano lesson, but she had certainly played in between: hymns and songs and musical games on tropical, insect-ridden pianos in every conceivable state of ruin. Her newly-revived piano seemed positively luxurious. Before long her daily chores included faltering scales and arpeggios and a tricky bit of beginner's Beethoven.

Quite soon after her arrival Miss Barbellion had acquired two willowy mongrels from an educationally reputable dogs' home. The family house was very large for one modest occupant and sometimes Miss Barbellion lay in the dark without her familiar mosquito net and wondered about the bumps and noises from below. She told herself not to be silly; on a thousand nights in tropical and unpredictable situations she had slept indistinguishably from a log and taken no notice of anything. The old house creaked and moaned after nightfall notwithstanding, and at the same time was full of memories of her large and once noisy family, and sometimes, unless she were tired enough to fall asleep immediately, she felt uneasy.

The two hounds (who, she afterwards decided, must have been just waiting for her arrival) were large but inseparable and she had no choice but to take both. The decrepit Victorian kennels in the back garden were soon restored to moderate luxury with the help of her team. Long-neglected grass provided a landscape that would have suited a pair of young tigers (with which species at one time Miss Barbellion had, of course, been familiar), and so was ideal territory for unobserved deeds. The two dogs were theoretically only allowed in the house if they behaved themselves and did not have muddy feet, but they were both so grateful to have been rescued from their drab, previous life that they were inclined to follow her around everywhere in appreciation. It was agreed between the three of them that walking in the street must not be over-strenuous. When Miss Barbellion took her bicycle – unless she sneaked out before they noticed – they would walk along beside her on the pavement, waiting for her chivalrously if they happened to pull ahead. In crossing main roads it was necessary for her to dismount and wait with them for the Green Man, because if she cycled across they would never wait until the lights changed for pedestrians but cross with her and they would all get in trouble. It was not that her hounds failed to grasp the rudiments of road safety (for she was a very experienced teacher), or that they were colour-blind, but they needed to be her constant guardians. Once in the park, however, they would lope off, leaving her to admire the hydrangeas and find a cup of tea in the cafeteria, which was always crowded with very young mothers and very new babies upon whom Miss Barbellion liked to keep an eye, for old times' sake. At a ring of her bicycle bell the dogs would report in to accompany her home.

There were many strange aspects to her new English existence as the uncertain summer passed. One major task was to write to all her correspondents to tell them of her new address. Many people in her position would have just had a pile of small cards printed and posted them off like wedding invitations, but to her it was a wonderful opportunity to write to her whole circle of acquaintance again. Her first letter was to Elizabeth, after an unusually long gap. To all Barbellions and descendants known to her she announced her repossession of the family castle, to which all would be chronically welcome, and told them that the family tree, now in danger of falling to pieces through sheer age, had been copied out with lots of extra room on a large sheet of drawing-paper now comfortably pinned on the kitchen wall above her breakfast table. Updates were always wanted.

Some had died without issue. According to her best knowledge, her youngest female relative was a thirteen-year old girl called Mina. Miss Barbellion had a very strong desire to meet this Mina, who was one of several unseen great-nephews and -nieces, for a certain particular reason. When Mina had come into the world her mother had written an excited letter full of exclamation marks to her far-distant Aunt Nancy to say that she had produced a baby *girl*, born ages after her brother Felix, who arrived on *February 29th*, because that year, 1972, had been a *leap year*!!!

Of course everyone gets excited about birthdays on that odd date, but the oddest thing of all was that Hilary, Mina's mother, had no idea at all that her own Aunt Nancy had been born all that time ago on exactly the same date.

Because of this fact, birthdays had always been important to Miss Barbellion. She had no interest in the stars or predicting people's fortunes; what she liked was people having unusual days for birthdays. Her slightly-older and best friend Cynthia had managed to be born on Christmas Day 1915, and they had exchanged vital birthday information right at the start of their primary school friendship, and felt themselves ever after members of a highly select society. When Miss Barbellion met Elizabeth at university very much later birthday dates had obviously not been the first topic of conversation between them, but she had been pleased to discover that her new friend had been born during a full eclipse while the whole country had come to a standstill to squint at the sky and shake their heads in wonder. Such a rarefied date qualified Lizzie, she thought, for inclusion. One curious fact about this minute secret fellowship was that Cynthia and Elizabeth had never met in person, and it was one of Miss Barbellion's plans now she was home to bring this about. Of course it was not certain that they would get on since they were all supposed to be crusty pensioners, but she thought that the Barbellion doll's house would come in very handy as an ice-breaker when they first encountered one another.

This large-size doll's house was a true hand-me-down. By the time Miss Barbellion had first come to play with it, a good sixty years earlier, it had become a rather ramshackle affair, and some of the features of the original house were hardly recognisable. Years and years before that it had come from a very expensive shop in London, a birthday present from another world for her oldest sister, Belinda Ann, who had finally died at the age of eighty-three after dozing uncommunicatively for years in a Home, far beyond any interest in things like doll's houses.

Belinda Ann and sister number two, Mary May, when on harmonious terms, had endlessly decorated and redecorated the rooms. At first their changes had been carried out with scrupulous care, all repapering measured and carefully cut out round the doors and windows and the patterns as neatly orientated as in a proud sitting room, but later standards had slipped and the interior decoration had become, it must be confessed, slap-happy.

a birthday present from another world

Considering its former importance to her it is surprising that Miss Barbellion hadn't thought once about the family doll's house since her return from afar, but as the close-stacked furniture that filled the top floor began gradually to disperse with the aid of her helpers the familiar old table emerged, and one angular protuberance under a dust sheet reposing on top soon proved to be the thing itself. Time was when her friend Cynthia had spent nearly as much time as she herself playing with that doll's house, and the idea of re-running the experience after all those years, just the two of them, was hugely appealing. A quick look revealed that the rooms inside were in chaotic disarray and not all of the furniture seemed to be there, but Miss Barbellion thought she might safely leave dealing with such problems until Cynth came to stay.

2.

Great-niece Mina lived with her parents and her older brother in a small modern house in Southampton. Miss Barbellion soon found an excuse that made it possible for her to go and call on them all one afternoon without a lot of fussing in advance. When she turned up at about 4 o'clock Hilary's husband Jean-François was out at work, Mina hadn't yet got back from school, and her brother Felix, she learned, would not be back that day at all. This disconcerted Miss Barbellion not a jot. It meant that there would be plenty of time to converse with her niece Hilary without interruption, which is exactly what she wanted, and then she would be able to talk to Mina.

Hilary responded at length and with unusual frankness in her aunt's company. Jean-François Brillon worked as a high-grade optician's technician and although he was approaching retirement he was hoping to keep working as they needed the income even though the house was small; somehow they had never really been on top of money things. Seventeen-year old Felix, not long before, had been handed some seductive leaflet by the careers officer at school about "seeing the world" and "dealing with dangerous difficulties in awkward places" as a professional soldier, and had more or less signed up on the spot. He had just gone off for his first bout of basic training. Miss Barbellion had to make do with a few child and young-man photographs. Hilary did not at all know what to make of this. No-one in the family had ever had anything to do with the army except when they had to and his father was disappointed and furious at the same time, but the boy was adamant. Miss Barbellion reflected that she and Felix looked likely to have much in common on the basis of his mother's description of his character, although his was a very different branch of service from her own professional life. Well, that may well be, but she knew too much about soldiers and what they often had to do to talk much further on that subject.

And what about young Mina, then? Well, Mina's speciality was lying on the floor of her bedroom and talking to herself (unless she had a pet mouse up there or something), and what she called 'playing.' Hilary didn't really know what to do with her. The girl had no proper friends, and spent most of her time incarcerated upstairs reading or drawing or day-dreaming. She did do her homework assiduously (which is more than Felix had ever done), and she was good at exams, but to tell the truth her parents were worried about their daughter. Why, she never ever –

Behind her Miss Barbellion heard the key turn in the front door lock and then the awaited Mina was in the room. She was a good bit taller than her great-aunt had visualised and too thin for her age. Miss Barbellion wondered for a moment whether she might be potentially anorexic, but the girl sat down at the table and helped herself to a biggish piece of cake straightaway, which was a good sign.

'Mina, this is your Great-Aunt Nancy,' said her mother. 'She has been all over the world and has now come back to England and wants to meet all her long-lost relatives.'

'I suppose I was the long-lost one really,' said Miss Barbellion.

'Hi,' said Mina. She put out her hand and they shook hands. 'I am pleased to meet you.'

Mina's speciality

She started on her cake, using the small fork neatly. Another good sign, though Miss Barbellion. Her mother poured her a cup of tea and asked,

'How was school today, Mina?'

'Fine.'

'What did you have?'

'Oh, the usual. English. R.I. Biology.'

Miss Barbellion inspected her great-niece over the rim of her teacup. The word "gangly" jumped into her mind, although on contemplation that was a bit unfair. Mina was fifteen years old, by her calculations. She bit her nails, she could see, and she could not but perceive the inner restlessness in the girl. When she looked up Miss Barbellion read intelligence and fire in her eyes in equal measure. There was a little further commonplace conversation. Miss Barbellion leaned across the table.

'Will you show me your room?' she asked.

Her mother made a fluttering movement and said something about untidy mess and things all over the floor. Miss Barbellion laughed and said,

'Oh, how did you know I was an inspector of tidy bedrooms? I thought my disguise was impenetrable.'

Mina laughed too and when they had finished their tea they went upstairs together. Mina's room, she saw at once, was much too small for her. In fact the whole house was too small in Miss Barbellion's opinion, although she was spoiled of course by the palatial quarters that awaited her in Bath. She had already made up her mind to invite her great-niece to come and stay with her in her house as soon as she could. She wanted to talk to her properly and show her things and give her some old necklaces and maybe go to London together to the art galleries and the theatre. There were drawings all over the floor. Miss Barbellion sat down on a big cushion to look at them. They were very dark and had consumed a great deal of black ink. Miss Barbellion thought them interesting but decided not to ask about them yet.

'Your mother tells me you have a rather intriguing birthday,' she said.

Mina sat with her knees clasped. She grimaced.

'I don't know why she tells everybody. She tells everybody everything. But I *hate* my birthday. Everybody says I'm a freak and born out of time and that I don't count and there are always the same stupid jokes about no presents this year and three years to go and all that. I hate it because it is all so predictable. Felix always goes on and on about it. It's not my fault. I wish my birthday was on any other day except that one.'

'What about Christmas Day?'

'That would be fine. I wouldn't mind that at all.'

'But that has its problems, too. My best friend ever, Cynthia, was born on Christmas Day. You can imagine the difficulty she had with having to receive her whole year's presents in one go? Her mother and father used to have to wrap her Christmas presents in reindeer and mistletoe paper and heap them artistically under the tree, while her birthday presents had to be in paper covered with doll's houses or –'

'Ballet dancers?'

'Exactly, a perfect example – and they had to be set out on the kitchen table as far away as possible from any sign that it was Christmas. And there could be no decorations in the kitchen. That was the birthday room.'

'So what was the problem exactly?'

'There were two. One was that Cynthia had to have all her presents for the whole year at once. And if they were good and proper presents (as of course they were), all that was too much. She was not an acquisitive sort of person. (Until she turned into an antiques dealer, that is.) And the other problem was that there was never a birthday to look forward to. With other children their parents could always say "Well, we'll see when it comes to your birthday," but she never had that sort of helpful option. So we used to commiserate with one another about our birthdays.'

'Why, did you have a problem with your birthday too?'

'Well, Mina, actually, I did. That is, I too had an unusual date for my birthday, but one year my father explained to me all about it and why it happened and after that I didn't mind anymore and actually I became proud of it.'

'But Auntie – or am I to call you *Great-Auntie*?'

Miss Barbellion hesitated. Her preference would have been to be called *Aunt Barbellion* as she might have in the eighteenth century, but she was unable to make the suggestion to the eager teenager before her.

'Oh, I think Aunt Nancy is fine; too much genealogy is a bit heavy going.'

'OK, Aunt Nancy, but what I wanted to ask you was what kind of awkward birthday could you possibly have? I can't think of any other type.'

'Well, perhaps I can let you into a secret.'

'I would promise to keep it absolutely safe.'

'I know that, my dear Mina, or I would not have even mentioned the idea. There are few enough people in the world who really understand what keeping a secret is. Shall I tell you what keeping a secret is, first?'

'Yes, as soon as possible.'

'You have to keep a secret so long that it goes off. Like eggs. If you really keep a secret properly, you never tell a living soul and it is still a secret when it cannot even matter any more. That is what they taught me, at any rate.'

'*They*, Aunt Nancy?'

'Yes. I cannot even tell you about them, you see. They are a secret too. But my really big secret that I am going to share with you is this: you and I, young Mina, share the same birthday date. I too was born on the twenty-ninth of February. But you must not tell anyone ever. No one in England knows it except Cynthia and Lizzie, and now you. Can you keep that secret?'

'I just don't believe it. You mean you were really born on that day in a real Leap Year like me?'

Mina was silent for a moment. What year could that possibly be, she asked herself. She could neither guess nor work it out. A hundred years ago?

'Feb. the twenty-ninth, 1916. A particularly fine Leap Year, that was, esteemed by connoisseurs.'

Mina was speechless. Then she jumped up and threw her arms around her great-aunt and squeezed her in her excitement. Miss Barbellion laughed.

'So much for now, young Mina. We can speak more about that later. I want you to come and stay with me at half-term. Would you like to do that? You can come down to Bath by train, can you not? I'll sort it all out with your Mum. Oh, and Mina,'

'Yes, Aunt Nancy?'

'Bring your drawing things.'

3.

It was certain in Miss Barbellion's mind that Mina was going to love the house in Bath and all the old things that survived in it. Beyond that she was hoping that her great-niece would feel at home and even come to see the house as a refuge as she grew older. A good start would be to find something particularly suitable for a Christmas present.

First, however, she would have to pursue Cynthia. They had spoken repeatedly on the phone, of course, and already managed to meet briefly in London, but now the house was ready it was time for the state visit. Their first meeting after her return had been such fun. Miss Barbellion knew that Cynthia would avoid a predictable 'how long is it since they had seen one another?' beginning to their first face-to-face conversation. She hated the 'Gosh, it must be 20 years' – no, I tell a lie – 24 years' dialogue that her long absence tended to provoke, because confusion was not telling a lie and it didn't really make any difference anyway. When she met up with Cynthia it was as if there had never been any interruption at all. What she had in fact bellowed across the street was: '*Barb*! Not a day older! *Absolutely* the same girl. Now you're back at last we shall do *great* things.'

As if by telepathy the phone rang in the hall. One of the dogs wandered out as if to pick up the receiver but Miss Barbellion got there first.

'That you, Barb?'

'It is I, Cynth. You are ringing, I trust, to announce the date of your long-anticipated arrival?'

'I was thinking of proposing around the weekend after this. Sort of Thursday-ish through Monday-ish? If that's OK with the staff?'

'Oh, I shall have released all the servants so that we can enjoy ourselves quite unsupervised.'

'And might the doll's house be available?'

'I think if you are well behaved and can manage all the stairs you will find everything ready for you.'

'Good. I have acquired a few bits and pieces for it since we met. An iron and ironing board, for example. We never had one before, did we?'

'No. Sounds deplorable when you announce it like that.'

'Yes, well I picked up a job lot of nice d.h. furniture too, some time ago. Quite old. If I can find it I shall bring it down.'

'How delightful. We will need some decent wallpaper; I'll have to see what I can find in one of the elegant interior designer's in town. A few choice off-cuts.'

'Splendid. I shall go and pack. Prepare for a weekend of resounding successes.'

After picking up necessities in the supermarket on the Tuesday, Miss Barbellion was half-reading the advertisements on the check-out notice board when her eye was caught by a plain white card on which was written SMALL GARDEN TOYS FOR SALE. LOFT FIND. BIG BOXFUL. MAKE ME AN OFFER!

There was no address given but the telephone number sounded local. In view of her recent doll's house conversation with Cynthia she couldn't help but wonder whether the 'small garden toys' might not be the miniature garden pieces that had once been her own favourite source of enjoyment in those far-off days, and she called up the moment she got home.

'I think we still have them...' said a woman's voice drily out of the earpiece in answer to her question. 'Yes, we do.

Someone did come to look at them the other day but they weren't interested. "Too fiddly," they said.'

'I see,' said Miss Barbellion politely. 'Perhaps I could come and take a peep, if that would be convenient.'

'Yes, whenever,' came the reply. 'I am here all day.'

Miss Barbellion wrote down the address; she knew where the street was and it was within easy reach of her bicycle. She sneaked out when the dogs were otherwise occupied and pedalled calmly off, telling herself that the toys would probably turn out to be plastic ducks for a garden pool, although 'too fiddly' did sound a bit encouraging, and underneath she was quite excited. She chained her bicycle to the railings and rang the bell. A plump woman in her fifties wearing baggy dungarees opened the door.

'Good afternoon. I have come about your advertisement,' said Miss Barbellion.

'The rocking horse? I am afraid that's gone.'

Well that didn't matter. Miss Barbellion had no need to buy a rocking horse. There was a perfectly good one upstairs in her playroom already.

'No, not that, I am calling about the garden toys.'

'Oh I see, you must be the lady that just called. I hope they are worth the trip. We found them in the loft, you see. We just moved in.'

She pointed to a capacious cardboard box labelled HOLLY'S GARDEN in faded ink capitals that was just inside the front door. Miss Barbellion knelt down, opened the two halves of the lid and peered briefly inside. The box was crammed full of pieces for making a miniature garden, the sort that could find a location very successfully by the side of a large, old-fashioned doll's house. Her heart was hammering with unabashed excitement. It was hard to believe. The pieces were all *plastic*, but at a quick glance they seemed to be the same sort of thing as her old version and there was lots and lots of it. She swallowed and stood up.

'Is that what you were looking for?' asked the woman.

'Well, in a way. Maybe. What price were you thinking of asking?'

Holly's garden

'Twenty pounds, my husband said. There's a lot of stuff there.'
That was perfectly true.

'They don't manufacture it any more, either.'

'I think fifteen pounds would be fair,' said Miss Barbellion firmly. 'I can offer you fifteen pounds.'

The woman hesitated and looked at Miss Barbellion. Then she nodded.

'OK.'

Miss Barbellion took out her purse and extracted one ten pound note and one five pound note.

'Here you are,' she said, 'the exact money.'

The woman found some tape and sealed the lid and corners of the box for her. Up on end it just about fitted on the front basket and she strapped it criss-cross in several directions for safety. Miss Barbellion cycled especially carefully so as not to shake up her garden treasure and where the road was particularly bumpy she thought she had better dismount. It seemed to take a long time to reach home.

It was good quality plastic, admittedly, but it wasn't lead. Her own cherished garden set, all those years ago, had been made of painted lead. The old box had been heavy, and she half-expected its new counterpart to be even heavier, but it was just the opposite.

That was a funny thing about lead toys, she told herself, seeing to tea, with biscuits all round. Lead was poisonous, everyone knew that now, but half their familiar possessions had been made of it: the soldiers, the zoo animals and her garden, deadly product of anonymous villainy, disguised by tasty paintwork to poison generations of innocents at play on nursery floors. But no one had ever heard of infantile fatalities due to lead, had they?

She nibbled a digestive convivially with the dogs while she thought about her exciting new purchase. There was very much more garden stuff than she had previously owned herself. This would be something she could enjoy with Mina. If she turned out to be that sort of girl, of course. Perhaps she would be put off if the first thing she saw was an old cardboard box with someone else's name on full of grubby pieces of coloured plastic. She would certainly need to clean all the stuff first and make sure there were no spiders or old razor blades lurking at the bottom of the box.

Bit by bit the pieces of miniature garden came out. Everything was dusty rather than grimy and in fact there were one or two spiders, but Miss Barbellion decided not to wash anything. It was better to have a go at each piece with a small, clean paintbrush, if only to ensure that none of the tiniest pieces went down the plughole. Water would be disastrous. The crazy paving was made of oblong pieces of unwashable cardboard painted to look like stone, and quite an assortment of other parts were still squashed in the packets in which they had come from the shop and had for some reason never been opened.

with a small, clean paintbrush

Laid out on the kitchen table her purchase turned out to be really something to work with. There was an assortment of trees, including three oaks, two apple trees, a silver birch, a weeping willow, a cedar and a poplar. Flattened underneath together with two ponds were also a fir, a pine tree and even a date-palm. Mixed up with these was a great collection of flowers, among which she identified with increasing pleasure crocuses, snowdrops, hyacinths, daffodils and tulips, lupins and delphiniums and a range of little rock plants with a rockery. There were roses and rose bushes, hollyhocks and sunflowers and even rhododendrons, her own favourite. Then there were brick walls and fences and gates, pillars and pergolas and plentiful sheets of lawn. To her delight there were also three garden sheds, two greenhouses with little plant trays, a bird-bath, a sun-dial, lots of chairs and tables and even a garden swing. And to do the work, a handful of planting tools.

Miss Barbellion sat at the head of her table and surveyed her new acquisition with a very great deal of satisfaction.

even a garden swing

There were many items for which there had been no equivalent in her old metal set; a lawnmower, for example, and the coil of garden hose. Well, it could not all live in the kitchen. It would all have to go upstairs and take root on the great playroom table. There they could be set out by Mina much like her old garden had been, side by side with the doll's house. There was plenty of room, which was lucky as she seemed to be sitting on a miniature Versailles. She could probably manage a front garden and a back one!

The tea-tray with its raised border was the most practical means of transport and there were going to be several runs. The dogs accompanied her halfway the first time and then left her to it. It was gloomy up in the playroom because Miss Barbellion usually relied on the overhead light and a couple of old standing lamps, but one now had a dead bulb, so she pulled up the blinds. It was already nearly dusk. One or two confused moths fell out onto the floor. Miss Barbellion placed the first tray-load carefully on the table, decanted the contents, and spent a moment spreading things out before she went back downstairs.

She thought she would just make a bit of a path with the flagstones, first a straight row and then a right-angle off to the right like she always used to, and one to the left, and tuck in a stretch of grass.

As she did so, an overwhelming wave of memory swept over her of a hundred afternoons at that table, following her own leaden paths through her carefully-tended garden beds, with fronds of greenery fronting bushes, and behind her one or two trees sheltering her one little building and the garden itself from the world outside. The same stools that had allowed the children to work on the doll's house gave an umpire-like posture for overseeing the whole, while a humped-back position allowed the eye to follow, as it were, from ground-level. There was always a secret peace to be found in her old lead garden, and Miss Barbellion had spent uncounted hours moving things around, replanting, displacing squares of lawn and her small pond like some Gulliver turned groundsman, oblivious to the others being irritating or interfering. Very often Cynthia was on the next stool to her, practising good housekeeping.

There was now a pleasant T-shape of summer pathways stretching invitingly to left and right. Geometry simply demanded that something else be added. The greenhouses were still downstairs but several of the first flowerbeds still had their little flowers in place, and before long Miss Barbellion had a convincing start on a proper garden well under way. Then it seemed silly to push things much further with most of the elements still waiting downstairs in the kitchen. Two more tray-loads, however, could by no means account for everything, and Miss Barbellion was considerably out of breath by the time the whole of her purchase was laid out upstairs, in tidy rows, ready for work.

4.

Miss Barbellion woke abruptly at first light next morning. She had been idling in a private boudoir where the sunshine played lightly across rectangular grey flagstones. Now there was an unexpected question waiting for her on the rumpled pillow: was there any possibility that her own old garden set might be lying downstairs in the cellar?

She could not for the life of her remember her father closing down the garden or wrapping up the pieces, but they had surely not been just thrown away or plonked on a bonfire? Maybe, just maybe, they were still somewhere in the house after all this time.

Miss Barbellion got out of bed in her agitation, and it was all she could do not to run downstairs and jump down the cellar steps at once. Then she hesitated. It was many years since she had been in the cellar of that house and she had probably never actually been down there alone. Now was not the moment to start potholing experiments. She shivered and got back into bed. She would have to get one of those tea-making machines that Elizabeth recommended. What would happen to old lead toys if they were wrapped up for half a century? Would they fall to bits or be covered in ominous white crystals, with any remaining paint flaking off in tiny fragments? She could not remember enough of her chemistry to be sure that some such disaster would not have happened. All that would be irrelevant, of course, if their old treasures had simply been consigned to a dustbin. Well, she would have to go down there after breakfast and check. As long as there were no rats. But the boldest rats would have withdrawn in the face of her resident hounds, surely?

Negotiating the Barbellion cellar was no easy matter. Her father's numerous deposits had been followed and overlaid by those of his various children. The consequence was that the explorer was confronted by piled boxes in profusion and items with painful sharp corners. She was looking for something, moreover, that might never have existed. How big would it be? What were the chances that it had a label, CHILDREN'S POISON: BEWARE!

Let us be sensible, she told herself. If this were archaeology the first things to be stored here would be at the far end; all the items from her father's time must be behind the later stuff, at the back where the cellar narrowed and the brickwork was lower. There was a grating that let in a little cool air, and a single light bulb that she several times bumped with her head swung to and fro. If this hoped-for box existed it should contain her garden and the animals from the ark (her father's favourite, and often a subject in his sermons), and many other things too. Such as all the soldiers from Tobias and William, and Samuel's collections, as well as the farm animals and the farmer's family. And the people from the train set. She could really not imagine her father throwing all that away, and now she came to think of it (she suddenly remembered) the lead African elephant with the wonderful ears had definitely survived on her father's desk where he composed his sermons; he would never have thrown away the other animals, surely? So, she was not looking for a hat-box (of which there were several) or a hip bath (in one of which she appeared to be standing). More likely an old suitcase. Ahead, rather encouragingly, was a number of them, with old labels and mouldy-looking straps, stacked neatly on top of two very old black trunks which looked as if they dated back to her grandfather or great-grandfather. She squeezed carefully forward.

The top suitcase was locked but not heavy enough. The next was green and yellow striped with many labels: Amsterdam, Venice, Vienna. This was much too heavy for Miss Barbellion's thin wrists, but it was not, on the other hand, locked. She clicked open the catches and raised the lid. Under the tissue paper there were many little packages wrapped in newspaper, sardined together so that the suitcase was nearly full. Miss Barbellion's heart was thumping with quite unexpected violence. What else could these be but the confiscated bundles of their childhood? Very slowly Miss Barbellion lifted the first parcel and began to unwind the old strips of newspaper. Her father, always unhurried and careful in what he did, had wrapped up his parcels like a mummy, first top to bottom, next left to right. Inside was an envelope of greaseproof paper. Inside that she found the station master, two porters and five or six passengers from the boys' train set. They lay in her palms looking back at her after more than half a century in unloved darkness. She felt, in the privacy of her basement, tears at her eyelids.

Her garden collection should be there too, then. Miss Barbellion swallowed. Recovery of this treasure would have to be done with Cynthia, she decided. This was no job for a lone aunt. She needed a strong right arm and all Cynthia's down-to-earth energies. Conflicting feelings persisted in her breast as she stood there still in the silent foundations of her lofty house. Voices with their echoes of tears and laughter broke over her again like sea spray catching one unawares. Feet running on the stairs, someone locked in the bathroom by accident, her mother calling them to bread and jam. She stood clutching the little railway figures and trembling slightly. Behind her she became aware of the two dogs, panting and clambering over obstacles, looking for their mistress. Were they anxious about her or just hungry?

many little packages

Well, she was definitely hungry herself. She picked her way laboriously back through the cellar to the stairs, holding the first parcel above her head like a recruit with a rifle wading a river. Eat breakfast and summon Cynthia. In that order.

5.

'Do I make myself clear? You must come earlier and stay longer. Come now, in fact. I have found the tomb of Tutankhamun.'

'Calmly, Barb. I have just woken up but I think I have taken the point. You are suggesting that I arrive in advance of our earlier arrangement?'

'Cynth, leave at once. I am going out to order a large supply of good food. And... wine.'

'Compelling. I will need a taxi from the station?'

'Most assuredly. Get the next train. I'll come to meet you.'

'Since it's you I will cancel all engagements. Expect me by nightfall. I'll come in the car.'

Cynthia might be, Miss Barbellion reflected as she lowered the receiver, a bit broad in the beam these days for investigating cluttered vaults. She had survived three husbands and each go had had its widening effect. Possibly the cellar would not be practically navigable for her. But there was no time to organise supplies and continue the excavation, and the supplies were obviously of greater importance.

'I don't believe this,' said Cynthia much later that afternoon. She was still in her coat, having demanded to see the doll's house the minute she came through the front door. Miss Barbellion had had a boiled kettle ready for ages so as not to be caught out as a hostess, but Cynthia's heavy tread plodded straight up the staircases one after the other with the two dogs, who apparently recognised her nature immediately, close behind.

'I just don't believe it,' she repeated a little wheezily as Miss Barbellion came through the door behind her. 'It's all here, isn't it?'

She laughed aloud, and took Miss Barbellion's hands in her own, and the two ladies embraced one another.

'Barb! I just cannot believe my eyes. But it must be so strange for you, living back here in this family pile. I can just see you teaching Sammy maths under the window while he wasn't listening.'

'It was chock-full of all sorts of clutter up here when I started, but as we gradually emptied everything out it all seemed to go back to the beginning. It was a great moment when the doll's house reappeared.'

'Actually this is your stool I am sitting on, isn't it?' said Cynthia. 'I always used to prefer the blue one.'

'It is still here. Do not panic.'

'Have you done anything with the house already?'

'No. I just had a look in the rooms and wondered where all the bits had gone.'

'Well, we can do something about that. I have something in my bag downstairs already, and I know lots of people who handle this sort of stuff. I'll make a few phone calls. Can't have the old place unfurnished now, can we? But what is all this floral-veggie nonsense over here? It's *plastic*, Barb!'

'You are right. I admit it. Plastic it is. This is my new garden collection. Picked it up for a song last week. I am hoping the old lead stuff might still be in the cellar. We are going to investigate that later.'

'I think I see why you needed help. It pains me to see the house in this way. Did you find any suitable wallpaper, by the way?'

all this floral-veggie nonsense

'No, Cynthia. We only discussed that idea the other day. But I shall.'

The stool sighed with relief as Cynthia got to her feet. She looked around again and laughed with pleasure all over again.

'Now, perhaps, tea?' she said.

Miss Barbellion had managed to get a date and walnut cake into the oven in time and Cynthia had taken the precaution of bringing a bag of crumpets, so a very great deal of hot tea was essential. The old railway personnel that she had already retrieved were now standing by the sugar bowl.

old railway personnel

When they were satisfactorily fortified Miss Barbellion cleared the table and spread sheets of newspaper over it to prevent lethal contamination of her regular eating spot by lead molecules. Her plan was to squeeze back through the cellar and bring up the mummified bundles one by one to be unwrapped by her fellow-worker. To do her justice Cynthia did venture down the first four or five steps like a reluctant swimmer dipping toes, but that, she thought, was probably quite enough.

'Oh my goodness,' said Cynthia, and she repeated similar utterances – some of which might have startled Reverend Barbellion – as the unwrapping proceeded. First to emerge were the animals for the ark. Cynthia was in paroxysms of excitement as she unwound each parcel, and kept saying 'This one's lost a leg,' and 'What a *pity* you don't have the original ark,' while Miss Barbellion patiently repeated 'but we *do*. It's upstairs, full of plastic animals from later. It's still there.' Cynthia muttered to herself as she dealt with professional facility with each package, tossing the newspaper aside in glee. Miss Barbellion left her to it and sat on the floor reading scraps of alarming headlines from 1933 from her father's morning newspaper.

There was only a handful of her original garden pieces, though, by the time the suitcase was emptied: a sundial, a bit of hedge and a couple of flaky bushes. The rest was nowhere to be found.

'I remember when you got the first garden pieces,' said Cynthia. 'Not these bits. A wall and some flowerbeds, wasn't it, a little shed and some path stones. And those rose bush things. You must have been thirteen or fourteen. It was a long time after we first played with the house. And once you got the first bits you were always after more. You used to sit and stare at that stuff for hours.'

'Wandering through a garden of bright images, you mean,' said Miss Barbellion wistfully.

'Sort of thing.'

'And Father must have decided they all had to go, the lead pieces.'

'Surely by then we must all have been immune to lead poisoning?'

'Yes, but by then the older ones had their own children, and they spent as much time upstairs in this house as we did. Remember, Tobias' wife had been a nurse before they got married; Paula, Paula Baring as was. It was probably she who read the riot act about "suitable toys." So they must have replaced everything with new plastic substitutes for the next round of children although nobody but I really liked miniature gardens so that got missed out. It looks as though

Father buried everything he could find down here with full honours and perhaps even a few suitable words.'

'Yes but your set was anyway only a handful in comparison with all that new-fangled junk upstairs. Maybe you ate the other bits?'

'A few rose-heads, perhaps.'

'Well I always thought those plants were too fussy and poky-poky to be really interesting.'

Their weekend programme unrolled of itself: food and drink, short walks, and dedicated work in the playroom upstairs. The new garden layout was developing beautifully. The lead sundial and the other historic survivors were given a place of honour.

'There is a pleasing disjunction,' remarked Cynthia, the following afternoon, 'between the orderly neatness of your miniature garden up here and the jungle that prevails below which in other houses would normally represent a garden.'

They were standing together at the window of the middle back bedroom which provided an agreeable view of the tangled greenery beneath.

'Many women of your age and disposition would be devoting themselves utterly to imposing order, trimming back here, sweeping up there, envied by acquaintances and relished by friends. And with what are we presented? No beauty to the eye, but raging nature in its cruellest state and ne'er a spot to perch the bum in comfort.'

Miss Barbellion laughed. The old garden bench was hard to make out, it was true.

'And that brings me to what is wrong with this miniature garden, at least to an outsider like myself. You've got tools and lawn mowers and lawn rollers and so on, but among all the green bits and pieces why are there no weeds? No scatters of autumn litter about the place, no cat poos, dead hedgehogs, prunings or smelly bonfires. It looks like a hospital awaiting a royal visit: everything immaculate, billiard table lawns, flawless flowerbeds and neat and tidy trees. It strikes me as poor preparation for a young person for the joyless, endless and fruitless nightmare that outdoor gardening really is.'

'Well it's not always fruitless,' said Miss Barbellion, sitting down again, unaffected by this treacherous broadside. 'We have delicious blackberries and raspberries somewhere down there; birds enjoy them in flocks every year. I believe several unusual kinds of apples can be found too. And anyway your argument is no argument. You may as well say that toy soldiers do nothing to prepare boys for killings and maimings when they end up in an army.'

'That is not a good analogy,' said Cynthia. 'Fighting on battlefields is fortunately not an everyday fate to which all boys have to resign themselves. Gardening, however, is.'

It was an odd thing, but all her lovely plastic trees were down the following morning, as if responding to Cynthia's critical blast.

Their collapse had made rather a mess of the garden plan as it was so far, and Miss Barbellion felt anxiously around all the windows and the eaves for a draught or leak to explain what had happened. There was no obvious explanation - which was comforting in a way - and with a patient sigh she set about righting fallen trunks and replacing flowerbeds and gate posts and put the strange matter out of her mind.

Just before lunch the same day, Cynthia plodded upstairs for another round of wallpaper removal and was much taken aback to find half her prized old furniture on the floor where she nearly trod on it, and she could only imagine that one of the dogs had leaped up on the great table, dislodging part of the treasures with a swish of its tail. She tut-tutted to herself as she collected up all the pieces. By the time she was back in the kitchen, however, cutting vegetables for salad and uncorking another bottle of wine, she forgot all about the disruption and chattered excitedly about other things altogether.

6.

The tall house seemed empty and inclined to echo its own noises without Cynthia's presence, and Miss Barbellion felt only too pleased that she had finalised the arrangements for Mina's arrival at half term. Work on the doll's house project was now well under way, but she was not sure what Cynthia was going to say if Mina wanted to continue the decorating herself. Cynthia planned to resume her status as Doll's House Superintendent soon – she had left full of promises about finding what they 'needed' as soon as possible, coming right back and fitting electric light in the rooms for a start. Perhaps Cynthia and Mina would even overlap.

Her isolation today was the deeper in that this was more or less the first time in her life that Miss Barbellion had ever found herself feeling conventionally lonely. As an adult she had never had, in the well-worn phrase, a moment to herself, but always existed in a context of abundant other people, most of whom adored her and all of whom needed her. Putting the house to rights had swallowed plenty of time and energy since her return to England, but all that was now over, and she felt the tug of an unfamiliar and unwelcome melancholy.

Time to write some letters, she thought. She turned on the radio and settled at the desk. Sister Marian, in Rangoon. Holy, funny and lethal at tennis. But her usually tireless pen would not respond even though in her mind's eye she could see the person to whom she was writing, of whom she was very fond. Well, I *am* out of sorts, she thought. Does this mean that after all this time I need a companion? Do I wish to be married, or take a live-in lady friend? Good heavens, no. Not for a moment. Oh well, she thought, maybe a spot of therapeutic gardening upstairs.

Cynthia had left the doll's house doors open so that the new wallpaper in the dining room would dry properly. Most of her imported furniture had turned out to be a good deal too small and a lot too modern; they would have to look into scales and proportions. There were shops that sold such things, and it was perhaps not so difficult to give the impression, as one's acquisitions were being parcelled up, that they were destined for a favoured granddaughter or great-niece, although experienced dealers probably saw at once through that kind of flimflam. Well, there was no denying that hers was a corking good doll's house, about as remote from the flabby, mass-produced items that were to be seen nowadays as modern flats were from proper Georgian houses. (Probably modern doll's houses suffered from damp, poor insulation, ill-fitting woodwork and subsidence just like their full-sized counterparts.) But it was unnatural that they now had the power to do up her quite sizeable doll's house almost in one go, and even a bit saddening. It was definitely one of the benefits of childhood, having to long for each new acquisition. As she daydreamed, Miss Barbellion found that she could remember with exactness the interior of the toyshop that stocked lead gardens; she could visualise the smart boxes under the glass of the counter with their paper labels, although she had never managed to get the expensive larger pieces for her own collection and had had to be content with the little transparent packets, one by one, of little orange flower pots or a group of colourful flowers to take home for planting. Nowadays original lead specimens would probably be very hard to find, but there was all her new garden to deal with.

Miss Barbellion pulled up her stool and set to work. It was true: miniature gardening was pretty fiddly. It required deft and thin fingers and good eyesight. She had noticed that Cynthia was constantly changing her glasses – she seemed to have three pairs going at once – and her fingers, though used to dealing with delicate things, were not what they were. Maybe that was the real reason why she refused to do any garden work, and drew such unfavourable comparisons with her own operations. Miss Barbellion smiled to herself. By the time she had finished no one would be in a position to speak disparagingly of her arrangements.

dealing with delicate things

From the beginning her new garden, despite its modern feel, worked the same tranquillising effect as had her original one all those years before. It was as if she had shrunk, Alice-like, all the while remaining perfectly aware that she was a grown woman perched on an uncomfortable stool and over-chilly. The slight discomfort of her limbs and back was insufficient to prompt her to move, but as her fingers busied themselves on the table Miss Barbellion found that her mind, far from being lulled into escapism, was still busily asking itself what its owner was going to do during her retirement. After all, all this could all go on for quite a long time, couldn't it? She was quite disgracefully healthy, slim and fit and looking like a woman of, well, rather less than her age. Maybe, if she could get away with it, she could even get a job. Phew! Now there was an idea! (One of the really useful items in Holly's box was the large plots of grass. Actually there were four or five. Miniature lawns. Wonderful. The old cork ones had been meanly-proportioned squares and there were never enough.) But this was a new problem for which all her previous experience left her unprepared. She found herself inside still a young woman, whose heart beat faster at the wind in her own trees, or a moment of kindness witnessed by accident, or even the majesty of her own father's church-spire stark against the sky.

So, she persisted, have I frittered away my quota of life? Should I have procured an adoring husband? Shouldn't I properly have my own children and, by now, their children? But only in the most self-doubting of moods could it be claimed that she had accomplished nothing with her years. She had saved lives, for one thing: grown men, swollen-bellied women and uncounted children. She could draw up a defiant report for the Angel of Death any time. But on this strange, lonely evening her unrestrained mind was blundering around like a maddened bull, undeterred that all broken china breakages must be paid for. She was the only one of her old school people (that is, as far as she knew) who had achieved neither husband nor family. There was no assessing what that might mean, however, unless she could bring all those girls together and take a show of hands to establish whether for all of them marriage plus children was still the only thinkable passport to happiness, and she knew that wasn't true. No. Being husband-less did not of itself

as her fingers gardened

mean being lonely: she was lonely now only for the whirligig of life where people turned to her round the clock for help and succour. That was presumably nothing like missing a dead husband, but by the age of seventy-one she might well have been widowed anyway, and many people in this country hardly ever saw their children or grandchildren even when they had them. So, then, what was all this wallowing, Nancy Barbellion? Inexcusable and boring. She had made her choice at the outset, had she not, realising with clarity that the conventional biography of her peers was just not for her. Well, I could always do a Cynthia and find a nice widower somewhere with ready-made descendants. She laughed aloud, discarding this unaccustomed insecurity in a moment. The millstone of someone else's whole family, overnight. And how they would come, anxious about nappy-rash, truancy, university entrance and marriage guidance, brandishing cuts and burns for her wee bottle of iodine.

As her fingers gardened and her mind flew about it came to Miss Barbellion that, probably, she really ought to have quietly carried on and eventually died in India. She had lived through all the episodes of a life of reputable worth and she had no business monopolising an empty family house which could accommodate many homeless people, several complete families at a pinch, or bus-loads of indigent students. Maybe that wasn't such a bad idea. A house full of students. They could discuss the meaning of life over communal breakfasts, walk the dogs and paint courageous murals.

Well, she would have to see. Whatever happened, she wouldn't be lonely when Mina arrived, that was for sure.

7.

Mina, of course, absolutely adored the house, right from her first glimpse of the green-painted front door. She was to stay for the whole of her half-term holiday and she loved every minute. The hounds provided a delicate welcoming committee; they were not all over her but offered their noses and submitted to tentative strokes and their owner caught them looking at one another as if to say "go easy on this one."

Miss Barbellion had allotted her great-niece one of the back bedrooms, which gave her a good view over all the interesting gardens behind the houses, including her own unrestrained wilderness. It had its own bathroom and had been prettily done up by the strolling actors. Mina was speechless as she laid her schoolgirl suitcase on the bed and stood on the rug before the little Victorian fireplace in which her great-aunt had set a vase of flowers. The room was perhaps three times larger than her bedroom at home, and was unmistakeable in its effect on her – one could see from the outside exactly what she was thinking. Miss Barbellion made noises about travellers usually needing a wash and herself making some tea, so that she could comfortably leave her alone.

Later she told Mina just to go off and explore the house, saying she could open every door and every cupboard if she wished as there was nothing to hide anywhere in the building, and of which other building in the world, she asked, could the same thing be said? The sound in the great house of her eager feet on the stairs and doors opening and closing made her great-aunt smile nostalgically. There was a lot to discover, but nothing compared to the unanticipated wonder of the playroom at the top of the house, and it was there that Mina was almost always to be found from that moment on.

The girl was instantly captivated by the family doll's house, and was so distracted by its interior that at first she hardly noticed the garden, but it was clear from her response that it too delighted her, and Miss Barbellion's fears that a girl of thirteen would be unmoved by it all were groundless.

Mina was not so interested in decorating the doll's house, however. What she liked was arranging and rearranging the furniture in the unfinished rooms, talking to herself the while, and she wasn't a bit put out that much of it was technically too small (or perhaps she didn't notice). She especially loved *drawing* the house, and the view up the stairs, or from inside, from different angles. On request she was given her own corner of the garden to arrange as most of the flowerbeds were still waiting to be planted and incorporated into the plan. She was happy to be alone upstairs at the huge table for quite long stretches of time, and Miss Barbellion even found herself reluctant to disturb her.

Their meals downstairs together were a delight, with long discussions. Mina was helpful with cooking and washing everything up, and all in all she was not in any way what might be expected from her mother's description. Perhaps at home she really was uncommunicative; in Miss Barbellion's house she was an excited chatterbox, full of enquiry and with a quirky sense of humour. On the second morning Miss Barbellion raised a serious issue over breakfast.

'This February 29th business,' she said. 'I know why it happens. Do you know why it happens?'

'No, Aunt Nancy.'

'Since it concerns you as well as me I imagine you might be interested?'

her own corner of the garden

'Of course I would. No one has explained it to me before, although I have asked several people about it, including one of my teachers at school.'

'I know what you mean. My father explained it to me when I was quite small. He said hardly any people understand how it is possible to have birthdays on February 29th and if you are one of the people who do, you have to understand properly why there are leap years. He said that everybody knows that it takes the earth three hundred and sixty-five days to go right round the sun, thus providing us with one year of time and seasons. The trouble is it actually takes three hundred and sixty five days *and six hours*, although do not ask me how they know that. This means that when they are arranging the calendar and allotting the days and months there is one whole extra day every four years, because four times six hours is twenty-four hours. This extra day has to go *somewhere* so they pop it on the end of February, which is anyway the most deprived month with only twenty-eight days, hence the possibility of our birthdays. If they didn't do this, after a while time would get out of sync. So I think we are rather important; we are the regulators of the calendar and without us everyone else would be in big trouble before long.'

Mina grinned. Pride in her date of birth was a new idea, for sure.

Over the week, though, even given that she was evidently a solitary person, Mina spent a slightly surprising amount of time alone in her aunt's playroom. Miss Barbellion felt that for a girl of her age there should perhaps be daily outbreaks of air and exercise and even mentioned that there was a good swimming pool nearby if anyone happened to be interested, but there was no taker. One had the impression, she thought, that Mina was preparing some elaborate plan upstairs. Part of it no doubt involved drawing, to which the girl was utterly devoted, but from what she let fall the pleasure of playing uninterruptedly with the great doll's house and the garden had captivated her entirely. As for the delights of Bath, Roman or otherwise, she had no interest.

'You have found all our old children's books, then?'

'Yes. I have read quite a few. They are much more interesting than the books I am supposed to be reading.'

'That is always true. Especially at exam time. Whenever you are supposed to be revising, the most awful rubbish becomes completely irresistible. Whose books are you expected to read, then?'

'Oh, Charles Dickens, Jane Austen, Thomas Hardy.'

'And have you actually read them?'

'I read *Jane Eyre* and *Tess of the d'Urbervilles* and about half of *Oliver Twist*.'

'What about Jane Austen?'

'I read most of, er – *Pride and Prejudice*.'

'Most?'

'Yes, well I somehow never finished it.'

'Didn't you want to find out who married whom in the end?'

'I suppose so. It just wasn't sort of urgent.'

'Well she's quite a heroine round here, Jane. I think we'll have to visit the Pump Room and the places she liked to walk and see if we can't persuade you to finish the story...'

By the Wednesday there were drawings all over the floor of Mina's room just as in her bedroom at home, and quite a few in the playroom too. Sometimes she and Miss Barbellion would talk about drawing. Mina exclusively favoured black ink and a wash technique; all her work was carried out in that format and she was completely disinterested in colour despite occasional pressure from her art master at school. She had brought plenty of her favourite ink with her but was beginning to run out of paper.

Miss Barbellion naturally always knocked before entering up at the top: at that moment she wanted Mina to come out to the shops with her. There was a good art supplies shop not far away, she said. Her great-niece was lying on the floor painting in the background to a view of Noah's Ark. She had drawn a tumultuous sea, with the high prow almost under water, hatches tied well down and the windows shuttered. It was affecting to see the accurate profile of their familiar Barbellion Ark transposed onto such a background. Mina had included a partly submerged whale in the storming waters, evidently reasoning that flood conditions would not require its presence on board for survival.

Mina jumped up at once at her great-aunt's invitation. In fact the shop proposal was really a pretext: she just wanted Mina to come out again with her, and the dogs, for a walk. So, off they all went, the hounds (who concluded that they were going to the pet-shop, knowing that their biscuits were running out) well in the lead. By common assent, though, when they reached the pet-shop, the hounds stayed outside on the street, so as not to alarm the feeble species that were for sale inside. Mina marched in with her great-aunt because she always loved watching fish in fish tanks and was in a sea mood. Miss Barbellion mentioned as they then strolled on that she had been hoping that Cynthia would be able to come down before Mina went home, but it didn't seem feasible. Cynthia, she reported, was extremely interested to meet this famous Mina person who liked doll's houses and even miniature gardens, but their meeting would have to wait to the next visit. They bought a large block of tempting drawing paper and more ink, just in case. Miss Barbellion made a light remark to the effect that her great-niece seemed to feel at home in her house, especially in the playroom.

'It is my favourite room in all the world. I never feel alone when I am in the playroom. It's strange.'

'What do you mean, Mina?'

'Well, it's like one has the company of all the children who ever played with those old toys somehow still being there, enjoying me playing with them. And they were all my own family. It is a nice feeling. Not like -'

She stopped and looked suddenly uncomfortable. Miss Barbellion smiled encouragingly.

'Well, I tried out your rocking-horse a few times on Monday but the one time I tried it properly it suddenly went incredibly fast kind of violently and I was nearly sick and it was very difficult to stop it. It was if it wasn't me rocking it at all. I cried out "stop" as if it were a real horse that could hear me.'

'How peculiar. And you didn't try it again?'

'Not likely. Nothing would ever persuade me to get on that horse again ever. It feels like it belongs to someone else.'

tried out your rocking-horse

'How peculiar. And you didn't try it again?'

'Not likely. Nothing would ever persuade me to get on that horse again ever. It feels like it belongs to someone else.'

'Well it is certainly the same old horse that belonged to us as children. That is a strange thing to happen. I should give it a miss, then. Perhaps you caught him in a bad temper, or something.'

'You are funny, Aunt Nancy. Maybe I'll do his portrait instead.'

'Good idea.'

One of Miss Barbellion's sea-going trunks was almost entirely full of plump, bundled-up envelopes, for she never threw away a letter that someone had written to her personally. Some of her most precious letters were written in dreadful, straggly characters by children who were the first in their family to read and write, often in honour of her own famous birthday (which she sometimes divulged), or that of the Queen. It was these letters that she wanted to show Mina. Some had little drawings, the church building, Jesus (mixed up with other heroes), or Miss Barbellion herself, thirty or forty years younger. There were also endless packets of small, black and white photographs, usually of mission houses, or mist over an African mountain, vast rivers and out-of-focus landscapes, and many sweet-faced nurses and nuns and Englishmen in shorts, the people in whose company she had spent so much of her life.

Mina was fascinated, even wide-eyed as she caught a glimpse of her great-aunt in those other worlds. Miss Barbellion was pleased in return to see how careful she was with the trunk papers, not trying to read bits of letters or dedications unless she was specifically invited to.

'No-one has ever seen inside this old trunk. It is like keeping all my memories safe and sound so I don't have to think about them, here in Bath. But if I want to, and I look at one or two of these, it seems that I have never forgotten anything. What a funny thing life is, if you just follow where it leads you.'

There was no sadness in Miss Barbellion as they pored together over the bundles. Her mission diaries were in a special tin box that she did not open, although she found that the idea of her great-niece reading them one day did not alarm her. What touched her most was that Mina suddenly said, looking up at her, that she would like to spend her life in helping other people. Unawares and in all innocence, she had echoed almost precisely the gentle advice of her unknown Great-Great-Uncle.

When it came to the final Sunday breakfast Mina was not at all happy. There would be school on Tuesday and her mother had made it very plain that she was to be home by early Sunday evening. Miss Barbellion looked up trains and connections and decided they really should be on the road so she ordered a taxi for twenty minutes' time. Mina had packed already, carefully stowing her beautiful jewellery box right in the middle of her case where it would be safe from all conceivable disasters. When they were in the hall Mina suddenly jumped up and ran upstairs. Miss Barbellion assumed that she had forgotten something in her room, but her feet clattered all the way to the top, and it was a good five minutes before she came back down again, rather white-faced.

Mina was uncharacteristically quiet in the taxi and still very pale when they arrived at the station. She stopped on the pavement and turned as if burdened with an important message. Miss Barbellion waited, smiling at her, but when it came to it the girl said nothing. As the London train pulled in and they moved up the platform in search of her carriage Mina stopped again and flung her arms tightly round her great-aunt and burst into tears.

'Hey, little Mina, there is no need to be upset. Your room here and the funny old playroom will always be waiting for you, and so will I. Do not worry one bit. Perhaps you can come back to see me during the Christmas holidays? Cynthia will be here then and we Twenty-Niners can teach her a thing or two about doll's houses, can't we?'

This was a good plan. Mina was soon restored to cheerfulness, especially when Miss Barbellion tactfully produced a packet of homemade sandwiches with two fizzy drink tins and an unhealthy kind of chocolate bar. Her great-niece sat by the window looking much younger than she had all week.

'Come back soon, little artist,' said Miss Barbellion, 'and send me one of your pictures when you have a chance.'

She disembarked and they waved goodbye in unison.

8.

Elizabeth Dean confessed on the telephone that she had developed a dicky knee and a journey to Bath right at that moment looked like rather an undertaking. Could Miss Barbellion possibly come over to Exeter instead? Miss Barbellion laughed and said she thought that would be perfectly possible.

It was a pretty cottage, as she had anticipated, the kind that provokes an appreciative remark from the passing motorist, and everything was in the strictest good order, inside and out. Miss Barbellion thought rosy apple cheeks and a floral pinny were needed to complete the picture convincingly, but her old friend was too thin and buffeted for that and she could not quite reply in kind when Lizzie declared how little she herself had changed.

Her room had a high narrow bed swathed by a heavy eiderdown with several rugs underfoot. It was stuffy but Miss Barbellion wasn't sure if opening the window was allowed. The garden below was immaculate in the early evening light and, for some reason, she imagined it covered with clean cold snow. For a fleeting moment as she stood there she wished she hadn't come. Probably their long-distant friendship would have largely been displaced by all the intervening letters with no face-to-face encounters. Miss Barbellion bustled downstairs with the box of continental chocolates that she had had specially wrapped, and to which she now felt absurdly grateful.

'I have a plan for you, Barbie,' said Elizabeth over the teacups, 'now you've got all this spare time.' So it was still to be Barbie and Liz. She would have welcomed Elizabeth and Nancy at this point, but there was nothing to be done to bring about the change. There was a proper fire in the grate although it was hardly cold enough to make it necessary. Elizabeth was dragging a large metal box out from behind the sofa. For a moment Miss Barbellion thought she was going to read her will.

'Do you know what I've got here?' she continued girlishly. 'All your letters. Every one. All in their envelopes with those colourful postage stamps from places I had not always heard of. I read them and re-read them and I kept them all. Yours are the only letters I ever kept. (I burned every letter from – you know – Sidney.) But your letters! All those wonderful stories, about delivering babies in a river boat, and the gun-runners with the runs who lost their ammunition and the giant slug in your nightie and all of them. Your letters used to make me laugh and cry and they were all so wonderfully long and detailed and I could never wait for the next one. I re-read them all again once I knew you were coming. And I have had a brilliant idea, Barbie. They would make a wonderful book. Everyone would love them. They are virtually a book in themselves already.'

Miss Barbellion's mind recoiled in horror. She leaned forward thoughtfully, as if considering the possibility, wondering about agents, photographic rights and a possible advance. What a thoroughly ghastly idea!

'Well, we'll see, Lizzie, we'll see,' was, however, all she could come up with. It had often been a useful prevarication, but in these circumstances perhaps too open-ended.

'And I was thinking,' continued Elizabeth blithely, 'that if you didn't want to do it I could do it myself. Edit them with a bit of explanation. It would be easy for me, of course. You could help with details, and maybe dig out some old photographs.'

Miss Barbellion made a firm mental note to hide her own letter trunk very effectively the minute she got home.

'I could easily put you in touch with my agent in London.'

An extremely convincing change of subject was necessary. Miss Barbellion lifted the teapot.

'Do you remember our old doll's house, Lizzie?'

'Vaguely. It was there when I came to you for the holidays that first year, when your father used to quiz us about theological definitions even though I was reading modern languages. Upstairs, wasn't it? I have never been much of a doll's house person; I never had one as a girl, and if you don't you never take much notice of them as an adult, I suppose.'

'True. Well, it is still up there. I have had fun recently with Cynthia putting it to rights again. Although a lot of the furniture is gone.'

'Ah, the famous Cynthia. So we are all starting all over again, then? You know, your father was a wonderful man, Barbie. I often used to wish I could ask him for advice, when I got in all that mess. Both my parents were dead by then, of course, and I felt dreadfully alone. But after they sent me to the Isle of Wight I was OK. "Wight as wain," the chap in charge of the home used to say, "We on the island will have you as wight as wain."'

'Father was always very comforting to people in trouble.'

'Yes. And not long afterwards I met Francis. So I burned all Sidney's stupid letters. Sixteen, no eighteen years of my life, blazing in the grate. I had the idea then to write something about foolish young women who squander their best years fruitlessly on married men but I discovered that there was abundant literature already on that theme and my agent wasn't at all interested.'

Miss Barbellion laughed.

'I know. But the worst thing is when you have to accept that your personal and private life with all its upheavals and traumas is just like the life of millions of other people, and that we are all part of a nation-wide soap opera. That is what is so interesting about your life – it is just the opposite in every way.'

'Well it was never boring, old Lizzie.'

'And I suppose I would have been a poor mother anyway. I am very impatient with small children. Not like you, with wards-full in an earthquake. You must have been amazing. Coping like that.'

'No choice. That sums up almost all of my experiences, Liz. No choice.'

As they washed up together Miss Barbellion found herself reinstalled as confidante, advising on what Elizabeth might have better done about her men friends thirty years earlier. Fortunately, her hostess demanded no matching biographical details in return, and, to Miss Barbellion's private amusement, had obviously decided long ago that her adventurous old friend was a maiden aunt and always had been.

Lizzie hadn't changed either, of course. Her old tendency to be just slightly humourless was still noticeable, but her company grew on her old friend, and she began to think it possible that their traditional friendship could come to flourish looking forward rather than backward. It was unclear to her how a meeting with Cynth would play out, though, especially since there seemed to be no common ground between the two of them and Lizzie was a self-declared non-doll's-house person.

After a late breakfast the following morning Miss Barbellion wandered out into the garden. It was easy to see how pretty it must be in the spring and early summer. There was a tidy arrangement with a shed and a small greenhouse, and she experienced a strange sensation of familiarity as she crossed the well-trained lawn. Eventually it came to her that the scale and neatness of it all echoed the small-scale garden laid out on her playroom table.

echoed the small-scale garden

How curious that was! Perhaps human beings in their houses and gardens with everything to scale and carefully set out in their proper places were toys too. Viewed from above, she thought, gazing up into the wintry sky, we are all one gigantic layout; houses, gardens, streets, train sets and farm sets. And she imagined the gods, for it would have to be lots of gods, watching their toys move themselves about (for they were advanced toys, and expensive), and wondering if they had the full set or whether more would arrive (which they always did). This idea was preferable, she thought, to Lizzie's cosmic soap-opera proposal. She pulled her Indian shawl tighter round her shoulders and soon went back indoors.

9.

What a funny weekend, thought Miss Barbellion, opening her front door, but I'm glad I went and I think we'd better get Lizzie inside this house in the near future. I shall discuss it with Cynth. We could throw a party.

Cynthia, though, would look at Elizabeth quizzically over one pair of her glasses and probably think her at once small-minded and irritating. Perhaps she was a bit of both. But that was not the whole story. Nancy and Lizzie had known one another for a very long time indeed, and their renewed contact had finally brought more laughter than she expected. One promising outcome was Lizzie's proposal that they should go on a very expensive cruise together one day. She had an idea for a shipboard plot, which Miss Barbellion thought rather inventive, and would be needing technical details and sea-going photographs for background.

The break had done her good, for certain: it was her first time of coming back to the house in Bath as home. More than that, and quite unexpectedly, the very solitude was welcome. She sat in the middle of the second staircase with her chin in her hands waiting for the dogs to calm down. They had been hysterical with relief when she collected them from the neighbour's garden round the corner; her earlier attempts to communicate that she would be coming back had just not got through and they had obviously been fearing the worst.

The Elizabeth trip had crystallised other things in her mind, too: she knew that her new life as it was suited her on a deep level. She would surely find something to do beyond the walls of her playroom of course, but there would be no husbands or companions. And, she thought as she climbed to the bathroom to wash off the journey and the dogs, there would be no autobiography either. She had read enough social history to acknowledge – when pressed by Elizabeth – that her collected letters might one day have interest beyond her own private memory, but she was not at all the sort of person to produce a book out of them. The very idea made her feel squirmy. It would be more appropriate for someone else to do that long after she was dead, when everyone concerned would also be well dead, and there might just possibly be interest in those strange souls who worked life-long for others so far from home in such unconventional circumstances. With that in mind she would somehow have to get her own trunk to the Society for their archives, together with the papers and photographs. They could take responsibility and she would tell Lizzie that she had done so.

A good decision that, once made. And 'authorship' could henceforth be put out of her mind.

Very much later, when all the occupants of the house were back to normal, Miss Barbellion went upstairs to find a place for the two miniature brass candlesticks that Lizzie had given her for her doll's house. They would look lovely on a mantelpiece over one of the fireplaces. The old doll's house, too, seemed to welcome her back in its own stolid familiarity, and the little candlesticks were precisely the right scale.

It was then that Miss Barbellion made a most disturbing discovery.

The huge garden layout that she had almost completed after so much time had been altered. Where she had preferred to spread out her flowerbeds as far as possible using the paths and lawns, things had been rearranged so that most of the taller flowers were now clustered together in the middle in

using the paths and lawns

what gardening books would call a "riot of colour." The changes had been carried out with a great deal of care; none of the flower heads seemed to have fallen off (which they were prone to do), and everything was neatly re-aligned. Miss Barbellion had to admit that the effect was pleasing, but the problem was she hadn't carried out any of the alterations herself.

And if she hadn't, who had?

There was no sign that anyone had been in the house during her absence, and anyway what kind of burglar would spend two hours redesigning a miniature garden and then leave without a trace?

Miss Barbellion flopped into one of the saggy armchairs and held her head in her hands for the second time that afternoon. Could she have got up during her sleep on Thursday night and carried out that work in an unconscious trance? She had never sleepwalked in her life and did not believe she had started now. Was she going batty? She got up and went for another look at the evidence. Her personal garden was certainly still there, but partly rearranged with the greatest care by someone else's hands.

She turned out the lights and went down to her bedroom to scrutinise herself in her mother's old mirror. She looked exactly as usual, no signs of senility, as far as she could see, or insanity. So what was going on? It couldn't be a trick cooked up by Lizzie and Cynthia behind her back, could it? Impossible! Cynthia had no key, and anyway neither of them could have carried out such delicate manipulations, Cynth especially. There was absolutely no one to whom she could turn to talk it through. Cynthia would accuse her of having a go at the drinks cabinet, or of somehow "making a mistake." There was no mistake. But a tot of something strong might be a good idea. She would have two tots, in fact. It had been a great shock. She ran downstairs, was outrageously overgenerous to the dogs, and took her healthy second whisky back upstairs to a very hot bath in which she re-read a large part of a favourite Edgar Wallace novel.

Miss Barbellion, clean and still slightly damp, lay back on her luxurious cotton pillows and closed her eyes. She breathed tranquilly. No further worrying was allowed: beauty sleep was in the offing. Then, bang! she sat bolt upright in bed.

A half-formed explanation had just come into her mind. She remembered the garden's fallen trees some weeks before, and then there was that strange remark made by Mina...

It was hard to believe that her explanation could be correct, but once thought of, it was even harder to believe that it wasn't.

10.

Miss Barbellion, therefore, fearful but resolute, got out of bed, put on her dressing gown and slippers, and went slowly back upstairs to her old playroom. She had left the door open before, and now she peeped hesitantly in.

It was then that she saw, paler than the moonlight that straggled through the uncurtained windows, the figure of a little girl standing at the garden table. She had long, untidy hair and was wearing what looked like a man's dressing gown with an improvised belt. She had bare feet and Miss Barbellion thought at once about proper thick socks: it was chilly under the eaves.

She stood frozen still, as one does when a garden bird settles unexpectedly close and can be scared off by the slightest movement, overwhelmed by seething emotions like a boulder in an inrushing tide. There was no need for any self-pinching procedures; she knew she was fully awake and fully aware of what she was seeing.

Nancy Barbellion was transfixed. It was one thing to have worked out a satisfactory theory on the basis of odd and unusual happenings, but quite another to have it confirmed by an ethereal being from another world, or, to put it plainly, a ghost in the attic. Miss Barbellion could neither move nor breathe, she was carved in granite. The figure had her back to her and was busy with the garden things, evidently quite heedless of Miss Barbellion's presence. Her heart was pounding at full pitch and she could still hardly breathe, until the turmoil of her feelings gradually became more manageable and sedate, and when she felt she was ready she retreated very discreetly and went back downstairs to her kitchen.

She sat quietly in the near-dark by her radio, whose dial gleamed with its steady green light. A wet nose nuzzled comfortably at her wrist. Obviously this must be the ghost of the garden's previous owner, whom she knew from the original cardboard box was called *Holly*. This Holly was definitely a ghost, at least judging by whatever Miss Barbellion had read about ghosts or been told about them. And anyway who else's ghost could it possibly be?

This, then, was the burglar with skilful, delicate fingers who could bypass two household dogs without being noticed to rearrange her flowerbeds to her heart's content. In fact, now she thought about it, Hounds 1 and 2 had both been avoiding the playroom lately, leaning moodily against the wall in the hall in a street-punk sort of way as she went by in the evenings. Maybe those particular noses had been aware of the being upstairs, knowing that their long legs and fierce expressions would have no power there. And, again, who else could it possibly be?

Phew!

She had certainly got herself a really unusual acquisition, had she not? She had purchased someone else's favourite possession in all good faith, a someone who could never leave it be, who apparently took a dim view of anybody else's playing with it and, specifically, disapproved of such a person's personal arrangement of it. What an adventure this was going to be! It was really something to swallow, that assertive dismissal of her carefully constructed and, indeed, beautiful garden arrangement. She thought that, once she had got used to the idea, she might try one or two experimental re-adjustments to the garden layout to see if she could discover more idea of the ghost's character.

Miss Barbellion turned on the radio, and the familiar, reasonable voice of the BBC World Service boomed in a welcome way round the walls of her kitchen as it had ten thousand times before in her life around the globe.

Hello, Nancy Rochester, it said, *this is the BBC in London and everything is normal.*

Yes, I know, but I have just seen a ghost in my loft, she said to the announcer.

But that same Nancy Rochester was not rendered wobbly or trembly by what she had just seen, nor was she discomfited by the thought that the wishy-washy schoolgirl figure was presumably still upstairs in her playroom. There was some proper story to be uncovered here; that was obvious. The little ghost had come into the house because of the garden box and could have nothing to do with her own family or history. (And there was an interesting thought, she told herself. She wouldn't have been frightened if it had been, say, the ghost of her little brother Samuel instead.)

Well, in that case she would have to find out about the history of that box, wouldn't she? This would mean trying to make friends with the ghost upstairs, while pursuing some rather interesting human detective-work downstairs, so to speak, at the same time. What fun indeed!

11.

She had Holly's last known address, of course, the house where she had bought the plastic garden collection. She reckoned that the girl must be (or was it must have been?) twelve or thirteen, and with that knowledge it should be possible to find out some real information. Miss Barbellion had a strong hunch that the more normal facts she had at her fingertips, the easier it was going to be to deal with the Presence in the Playroom.

She therefore telephoned her solicitor (who had been much struck with her during their brief professional contact over the transfer of the house, and was exceptionally pleased to hear from her). In his view the details that she did have (which she outlined theoretically, as if she were writing a detective story) would amply suffice for her to identify the girl and her family in full and lead her to birth, marriage and death certificates and any other plot elements without difficulty. The place to go was a Record Office in London, where they were always very helpful to professional men and women (although there might be a modest fee), and he closed by indicating that he would be very pleased to help with any legal issues that might arise during composition, and glad to put his name down for a copy of the final publication.

Miss Barbellion accordingly took a train to London the next morning. With the help of a slightly grumpy clerk who clearly doubted that she was any kind of professional, she established by tea-time that Holly Minchin Hocks had been born on February 29th 1956, and that she had lived with her parents Gregory and Sandra Hocks at no. 47, the house she already knew, as their only child. She had had the misfortune to die very young of pneumonia with complications. The date of this dismal event was also carefully recorded in the coroner's exact script: February 29th 1968.

Miss Barbellion gladly paid her fee and folded the thin sheets of paper thoughtfully. She made her way to Paddington still wrapped in contemplation, and treated herself to a mediocre cream tea at the railway tea shop. She was in no state to criticise the scones, however. It must all be true, then, she thought. I was right.

Oh my goodness.

There was a letter waiting at home from Lizzie. It was written on violet paper with small flowers in each corner. All her previous letters had been on flimsy blue airmails:

Dearest Nance,

I was so happy to see you here after all those long and complicated years and await a repeat visit soon. It was just smashing to see you. Maybe we should think of going back to Oxford together to do another degree? You can do Chemistry at last and I rather fancy the idea of Anglo-Saxon.

Meanwhile (don't be cross with me!), I have spoken to my agent, who is absolutely dying to take you for an expensive lunch in Kensington to discuss your book, which he is convinced will be a sure-fire success.

He thinks it could be called Travels with my Blackboard. *Perhaps I shouldn't have referred to your book quite so prematurely as ideal material for a film. I said I would pass on his message, but I promise I won't take it any*

*further now without your say-so. Also, my knee (about
which I have been so rude) seems to have decided to be
cooperative again and I would love to come to Bath for
a few days soon to see what you've done with the real
house (and the miniature one).*

*I am going to start another book now - you have quite
cheered me up.*

As always,
Liz.

her knitting bag

Well, that was a surprise, and Miss Barbellion was pleased. This seemed the right moment, then, to swing the first full meeting of the Bizarre Birthdate Club. What would happen if the three of them really did manage to get together?

Dearest Lizzie [she wrote back],
Come here as soon and whenever you can, on condition that the expensive business lunch is for you to discuss your new book, and that you forget all about mine.
I will see if we can get Cynthia to come down at the same time, perhaps.
Likewise yrs.
NRB

She smiled to herself and tucked the letter in her knitting bag for safety.

12.

Miss Barbellion rang the Carnarvon Avenue doorbell without rehearsing what to say. The same lady answered.

'I am sorry to trouble you,' she began, 'but you remember perhaps selling me the miniature garden a few weeks ago?'

'Oh, hello. You again. Is there a problem? I don't think we can take it back now.'

'No, it's not that at all. I am very happy with it all. I just wanted to ask you whether there happened to be any other toys in the loft when you moved in?'

'Only the old rocking-horse that was already sold. I think I told you that before.'

'Can I ask you what it was like?'

'Well, it was old and beautifully carved. It was fully painted too, and with a proper tail. It brought Gordon some luck. It had the name painted on the side, and there was a horse with the same name at Kempton Park. He won a bundle. After that, though, we sold it. It took up a lot of room.'

'Can I ask you what the name of the horse was?'

'I'll never forget. It was Hollyhocks.'

'What a lovely name for a horse. I would have bought that for young Penny, too, I think,' said Miss Barbellion, sounding rueful.

'It was a lot of money, mind you,' came the reply. 'Four hundred pounds. Old ones always fetch money. Actually, it made Gordon think we should go into the second-hand rocking horse business. He thought we could buy up old fairground horses and convert them. Got quite excited about the idea.'

'Gosh, that would have made such a wonderful present for my niece. Do you think there is any chance that the new owner might part with it?'

'I have no idea. You could always ask him, I suppose. I've got his name and address written down because of the cheque. I'm always very careful with cheques. But what would you say? He might be rather put out.'

'Oh, I shall think of something. He won't mind. He can always say no.'

'He was a Mr Barber, I think.'

Write or phone? Miss Barbellion asked herself, as she walked thoughtfully back down the path. Neither, she decided. She would simply go round and see him.

Miss Barbellion tried Mr Barber's doorbell later that afternoon. A worried-looking man in his early sixties came to the door and looked at her inscrutably.

'Hello,' said Miss Barbellion. 'I've come about the horse.'

The man nodded.

'I've been rather expecting that someone would come sooner or later. Please come in.'

Miss Barbellion chained up her bicycle and wiped her shoes politely on the mat. She followed him into the kitchen. He stood by the sink.

'Have you come to take it away?' he asked.

She expected him to offer her coffee or something. It was the sort of moment when people do. There was a curious sense of reluctance about him. There was a pause.

'Can I see the horse, do you think?' said Miss Barbellion.

'Yes. Oh yes, of course, you must. It's upstairs in my son's old room. We... bought it for the grandchildren.'

'Of course you did.' She nodded, understandingly, and followed him into the hall and up the stairs.

The curtains were drawn and the horse was suddenly immense and startling in the gloom of the small chamber, a captured dragon. The staring, painted eyes seemed to acknowledge her with recognition; she half-expected a twitch of the nostrils or a whinny. The horse was heavily laden with thick encyclopaedias and fat dictionaries piled high on his back and strapped in position. Then she noticed the iron bars jammed and chained rigidly between the runners.

the horse was suddenly immense

'It rocks, then, does it?' she asked quietly.

The man nodded. He was still halfway in the doorway as if ready to bolt downstairs.

'On its own. Sometimes all through the night. My wife wears these grotesque headphones in bed in case it starts. She asked me a hundred times to make a bonfire for it and chop the thing up with my axe. But I paid a good deal of money for that horse. We thought it would become a family heirloom.'

'It's probably in the wrong family to be an heirloom,' said Miss Barbellion.

'That I agree with,' said the man. 'So what, may I ask, do you propose?'

'I think I must take it away to a good home,' said Miss Barbellion. 'That will be the best solution. I will, of course, pay you in compensation. Can I ask how much you paid for the horse?'

'Four hundred quid. Seemed a respectable price – I looked into it first. Right now, though, you can have the thing for two-fifty. I would be pleased.'

'No,' said Miss Barbellion in her firm way, 'I shall pay you the same amount that you paid. That is the fair thing to do.'

The man was silent after this statement.

'You know something about this horse, don't you?' he said at length.

'I think I know what has to be done.'

'It's a generous offer, I must say,' said the man.

'I can give you a cheque here and now,' said Miss Barbellion, 'if you agree, and if you could get it delivered it to my house. I don't think it will fit in my bicycle shopping basket.'

Mr Barber laughed. She could almost see the tension of the last weeks draining out of him.

'I'll get Peters from next door. He's got a van. He helped me when I bought the thing.'

'It's on the fourth floor, I'm afraid,' said Miss Barbellion. 'Lots of stairs.'

'Frankly,' said the man, taking the cheque and reading it over, 'I don't mind if you want it delivered to the roof. As long as it is out of this house. We'll be there at 7 o'clock tonight if you will tell me the address.'

'What a strange place,' said Mr Barber's neighbour, looking appraisingly round the playroom. Both men were sweating heavily; it had been a brutal job on the staircases notwithstanding his neighbour's earlier remark and they had gouged the wall in two places. Everyone paused. Mr Barber noticed the other rocking-horse which was standing across the room under the eaves where Miss Barbellion had pushed it out of the way.

'You a collector, then?' He looked at her suspiciously all of a sudden, as if a bargain had slipped from his fingers and she was going to make a killing the minute he went home.

'Oh, no,' said Miss Barbellion, 'I am not a collector. Not by any means.'

'This horse here is something in comparison with your old one. Size and carving and everything.'

'Oh, yes,' said Miss Barbellion rather loudly, in case anyone was listening, 'this is the most wonderful rocking-horse I have ever seen. Whoever owned it originally must have been very fortunate.'

The two men removed the two rusty bars that still jammed the runners and Mr Peters shouldered them with a grunt. Miss Barbellion followed the two men down the stairs all the way to the front hall.

'Well I am glad to see the back of that, I can tell you, and I wish you luck with it. If you understand me.'

Miss Barbellion nodded and they shook hands and the two men left.

She wondered how soon it would begin. It would be dark in an hour or so. She felt excited but not at all nervous.

Miss Barbellion boiled an egg for her supper with some

bread and butter followed by two plums and a cup of black tea. She wrote several letters and discovered she was running out of envelopes, so she made a note to that effect on her shopping pad. After that she washed up and listened to the news on the radio. By then it was quite dark. She got herself ready for bed and put on her dressing gown and slippers with an extra jumper.

Very quietly indeed Miss Barbellion went up her staircase, floor by floor. She had learnt many years ago how to achieve that feat in perfect silence and she had lost none of her earlier skill. This meant that, as she approached the door to the playroom at the top, there were no sounds from underfoot that might compete with any noises that might be detectable from the other side. She sat down on the top step very carefully indeed and listened, her heart beating loudly.

And then she heard it, unmistakably, from the other side of the familiar door, the creaking to and fro of a heavy old wooden rocking horse.

13.

As she expected in the bright sunlight of the following morning, nothing further had been interfered with in the miniature garden. Her visitor was obviously more interested in riding her horse than tending her flowerbeds, and it struck Miss Barbellion that she probably had only come to play with the garden in her playroom after the horse had been put out of action in the other house. Of *course*, said Miss Barbellion out loud, her thoughts coming quickly, then everything makes sense. Holly must have had uninterrupted access to the loft of her own childhood home all the time that her garden and her horse were stored there, but when Gordon and Co. moved in, despoiling her refuge and selling everything off, all that came to an end.

So that was it, then: she had a resident ghost. Nothing to worry about there, could happen to anyone. In view of her discoveries there could be nothing to fear in this arrangement, and she found that she still wasn't at all disturbed by it. It seemed to her that the best thing was to leave her ghost to its own devices for a day or two, and when she felt the moment was right she would take things a bit further. She was extremely curious as to whether she would be able to communicate with Holly.

It was, therefore, not until the Friday evening that Miss Barbellion went upstairs again after dark to listen for the creaks. Creaks were certainly to be heard, and they were louder and more vigorous. Miss Barbellion opened the door as quietly as possible and stood without moving in the doorway.

she tried a wave

Across the room the old painted horse was rocking forwards and backwards to its fullest possible extent. In the saddle, her knees gripping the flanks and her hands lost in the flowing mane sat the little girl she had seen before. She had the same peculiar lightness and wispiness about her as if a strong puff of wind could instantly unseat her and blow her away. When she saw Miss Barbellion in the doorway the girl stopped rocking and the wildly swinging horse gradually quieted itself into complete stillness. There was total silence. They looked at one another in the streams of moonlight from the tall windows.

'Hello, Holly,' said Miss Barbellion at last in her clear voice. 'Welcome to my playroom. You can come and ride here on your horse whenever you want. That is why it is here. It is a wonderful horse and you are a lucky girl.'

There was a very long silence.

'Can you hear me, Holly?'

There was a small but undeniable nod.

'That is good news. In that case I shall leave you in peace for now, but one thing I want to ask you is this: you do understand that I brought your horse here for you?'

There was another nod.

Miss Barbellion smiled, and before she departed she tried a wave. After an interval the girl waved back, a small sort of wave that did not last long, but a wave nevertheless.

14.

Miss Barbellion made up her mind that the best way to promote more satisfactory communication with Holly was to act from now on as if everything was perfectly normal. The next time she heard the horse in action she knocked at the playroom door with one knuckle to give her warning and went straight over to her garden table, waving a casually friendly hello as if she were arriving at her office for work. It was now some time since she had done anything on her garden. She wanted to put more things back as they were and the second greenhouse needed stocking so she pulled up a stool and got to work. She was fully intent when she became aware that the horse had fallen silent, and looked up to see Holly standing at the far end of the table.

'Do you prefer your old bits of garden or mine?' asked Holly.

Her voice, now that she let it be heard, was not echo-ey or full of 'whoo-whoo' effects, but diffident, and, if anything, a little rusty through disuse. She didn't bother with preliminaries like "Good evening" or "How are you?" and Miss Barbellion had the feeling that she never would.

'Well, I suppose my old one, really, although there's not much left to play with. It brings back many memories for me.'

'Is your name Leila?'

'No. It isn't. It is... Nancy. Most people call me Miss Barbellion.'

'Oh. I found a book up here with that name in.'

'She was my sister, but she died recently.'

There was no response. I suppose, thought Miss Barbellion, one can hardly expect a ghost to react sympathetically to news of someone's death; it would be hypocritical for them to say, "Oh, I am so sorry" wouldn't it?

'Your own garden pieces are very heavy, aren't they, Nancy?'

'They are. They are made of lead.'

'I see. How inappropriate for playthings. And how strange they seem. Do you ever ride your horse, Nancy? We could have a race. Not that yours is much good for riding. His tail needs attention, by the way. As do other features.'

'No. Not really. At least, not the way you do. I have a little see-saw go now and again when I fancy.'

'I think we could beat you easily.'

'I am quite sure you are right. But I have ridden a full-size Arabian stallion in my time, and jolly fast he was too. I had to hold on like you do, for dear life.'

'Well I never had that chance. Just ponies at the beach. That is all. I learned to ride properly with him.'

She pointed vaguely over her shoulder.

'Tell me, Holly, did you get all your wonderful garden pieces in one go, or bit by bit, like me?'

'Oh, bit by bit, of course. Weekly pocket money, birthdays, or if I was a specially good girl. They bought me a lot more when I was ill. Actually they tried to get me the whole set then, but I never really used most of the new pieces. Gardens things are no good when you are in bed. They get everywhere. I used to keep the people under my pillow, though, the garden people.'

'Well, you certainly ended up with a much bigger collection that I did. Most of mine seems to have got lost.'

'They probably took the lead for bullets.'

Miss Barbellion laughed.

'Did you have lots of dolls and things too?'

'Of course I did, but after my Tragic Death they were all burned. In case they were infectious. My garden and my horse escaped and went up in the loft. Fortunately.'

She sighed.

Miss Barbellion decided to relocate one of the ponds. That meant moving quite a lot of vegetation and some path too. Holly watched her with a seasoned eye.

'Nancy?'

It was really quite difficult for Miss Barbellion to swallow being addressed in that fashion. There was literally no other person in the world who called her straight out by her first name. Cynthia called her by one dreadful abbreviation and Lizzie by another. But she could hardly stand on ceremony here in her own playroom in conversation with a dead girl's ghost. She had given a strong hint about it already. She would sound like the worst sort of school-ma'am.

'Yes, Holly dear?'

'Do you know what I am?'

'Yes, dear. Of course I do.'

'Well, how come you didn't scream or faint or anything when you first saw me the other day? I was truly surprised, frankly. I saw your reflection in the window, as you no doubt realised?'

'I do not understand your question, Holly. There is nothing about this situation that surprises me. Why should that surprise you?'

'Well, do you believe in ghosts, or did you before all this?' She waved her hands about, meaning their situation, here and now.

'Of course. I have always believed in ghosts. I have the idea that everyone believes in ghosts underneath, although not everyone will admit it.'

'Well, doctors don't, do they, and scientists?'

'Not on a summer's afternoon, maybe, but after midnight in a ruined church on a Yorkshire moor a good ghost story gives even scientists the heebie-jeebies. It is easy for people in white coats and laboratories to be sceptical. Men and women have believed in ghosts since the very beginning of time. Since they danced around in caves. Tell me, Holly, did you believe in ghosts before you – er – died?'

'Of course I did, Nancy. Everybody I knew did. Except Uncle Simon who didn't believe in anything.'

'Also, when people here talk about whether they believe in ghosts or not they only consider it from the position of their own experience in England, but people all over the world believe in them. I could tell you of things I have –'

Holly held up her right hand.

'Please, Nancy, not now.'

'Sorry, I thought, as we were having a discussion, that –'

'No. Nancy, why do you have those horrible dogs?'

'They are thoroughly sweet-natured, my hounds. You do not understand the situation. I need them to feel safe.'

'From intruders like me?'

'I was thinking of more solid types. They would run for their lives if they saw you, Holly. I notice they never come up here in the evenings any more. We used to do jigsaws together. Do you think they would be able to see you if they came in?'

'I cannot tell.'

'Have many people apart from me have seen you?'

'I think none. I made sure that dreadful Barber man never actually saw me. That is what drove them to distraction. If they had seen me in the saddle they would probably have been relieved that there was a physical explanation.'

'Yes, I can understand that. So why didn't you hide from me?'

'I knew you were different. You rescued the horse and brought it here to this perfect place.'

'That is good, then. Are there lots of ghosts like you that come back like you?'

'I am not allowed to answer that type of question.'

'Oh, I quite see that.'

those horrible dogs?

'But what I can tell you is that the ones who do come back have a trouble. That's what makes them do it.'

And with that she turned on her heel and ran back to the horse. Miss Barbellion decided it was time for bed and blew her a goodnight kiss.

'Sweet dreams, Nancy' came the voice behind her as she quietly closed the playroom door. She went thoughtfully downstairs.

15.

'Nancy?'

'Yes, Holly?'

'Why aren't you married?'

'That is a slightly personal question, isn't it?' said Miss Barbellion. She had only come upstairs for a minute.

'Well, aren't we close friends, Nancy?'

'In a way we are, but I would never dream of asking you such a question.'

'Oh, I don't mind, Nancy. I have never been married. I died too soon. There. You see how easy it is to deal with personal questions?'

'Well, I have never been married either,' said Miss Barbellion.

'Why not? You aren't that bad looking. For your age, I mean.'

'Thank you, Holly. The truth is, I never met a person to whom I wished to be married.'

'But the world is full of perfectly nice men, isn't it?'

'Certainly. About half full. And I have known a great deal of wonderful men in all shapes and sizes. Actually, quite a few of them asked me to marry them.'

'What, all at once?'

'No, they queued up. Some preferred moonlight, others

a table in a good restaurant. On one occasion it was during the first interval of a long opera in Milan. Then there was an American who asked me to marry him when we were under fire in Cambodia. There were lots, now I think back. They were all smashing men, but I never really had time for getting married. And my work often meant that I had all the children I could possibly want. Sometimes twenty babies with only one helper and no clean water. So I just never had time to fall in love and get married. And then all of a sudden I was over seventy and on a boat back to England. Actually there was a man on that boat who asked me if I would like to get married. So I have never been short of suitors.'

'Crikey,' said Holly.

'And I am now happy to be an aunt, a great-aunt, and very possibly a great, great-aunt too. There is plenty of life left in the Barbellion tree.'

'Well,' said Holly, 'if I had lived as long as you have I would definitely have married some of them. Three or four is about right. Men usually run out of oomph, and women who don't have to get a new one. That seems to be the rule.'

'I see,' said Miss Barbellion. 'Any other questions?'

'Yes. Are you rich?'

'I have enough for my needs. I can buy the occasional Victorian rocking-horse, for example, and I own this house and I have my pension. So I don't have to worry. You don't have to, either. I shan't sell your horse.'

'We weren't rich at all. Hollyhocks came to my Mum in a will from some rich branch of the family. Father said it was typical of them to put everything on a horse that would bring home nothing. Mum loved it; she spent half her pregnancy riding on it, gently of course. So that is why I am a natural horsewoman.'

'Yes,' said Miss Barbellion politely, 'it does show, the way you sit.'

'Posture is all for a girl,' said Holly.

The phone was ringing below. Miss Barbellion went down and just caught the call in time. She would have to train the dogs to bring her the receiver or get an extension put in.

'Barb! It's me. Everything ok there?'
'Certainly. High spirits here, I think I can say.'

another bag of swag

'Glad to hear it. Have another bag of swag for you; a load of old furniture. There's a grand piano and a lovely three-piece suite. Can't wait to try it out. Oh, and a great load of plastic garden stuff has come in, too. There's a lot of that to be found. If you want it all, that is?'

'Need I answer that?'

'As I feared. Will be back soon.'

'Wonderful. You know that you are welcome here just as soon as you can get here. By the way, Cynth, since you're supposed to be finding lead items, any chance of some trees? We are very poorly off arboreally speaking.'

'Forget it, Barb.'

'What kind of defeatism is this?'

'I already asked people, as a matter of fact. A woman who does fairs told me some blackguard in the Midlands buys every lead tree he can get his hands on. He keeps them all on his mantelpiece in his sitting room, and has built a special extension enabling him to reproduce the New Forest in miniature. Every tree that surfaces seems to end up there.'

'This is gluttonous and unfair. Hog-like, in fact. Are we never to secure our English oak and Lebanese cedar?'

'I am pursuing lead vegetation in each cardinal direction, Barb.'

'We should get ourselves invited there for tea and sneeze as hard as we can and watch them fall over, row after row, like dominoes.'

'We will overcome, never fear. Plastic trees are easy, meanwhile.'

Miss Barbellion knew it was time she did something about the dusty playroom blinds. She thought about it again, back upstairs, while sitting in one of the playroom armchairs. She inspected the tips of her shoes, which needed polishing.

'Who was that?' came the voice from behind her. Holly was lying on her back on the floor.

'Just a friend.'

'I see. Cynthia, perhaps?'

Miss Barbellion felt a little put out by this remark but said nothing.

'Have you practised today, Nancy?'

Miss Barbellion stretched in her chair and put her hands behind her head.

'I have to say that the secret of learning the piano is daily practice.'

'Yes, Holly,' said Miss Barbellion. Actually, she hadn't practiced for several days now. What with one thing and another she hadn't felt –

' – and when I say practice,' continued the voice, 'I don't mean just playing over what you can already do. I mean working at the other bits. Over and over again. That's what practice means. I am a bit surprised that it is necessary for me to say this. Piano lessons are not cheap when you start to add them up, and you have rather a long way to go, considering your age. How old are you anyway, Nancy?'

'Holly you are frankly impertinent. In subject of address and manner of address alike. I do not need you to supervise my piano lessons.'

'I'm sorry but I think you do. I was already Grade 4 when I had to stop. And how do you think I achieved that? By practising each and every day. I came home from school, changed out of my uniform, had a biscuit and a glass of milk and sat down on my piano stool. And that is what you should be doing.'

'I don't like milk.'

'That part is not so crucial. And that Beethoven thing is not so difficult. You are making very heavy weather of it all.'

'Holly, if I may say so you are being quite unpleasantly ill-mannered. I do not need this kind of intimidation, and I do need my privacy to be uninvaded.'

'Well, that may be so, but sound travels in an old house like this and it is scarcely possible for me to be unaware that you have not done your practising.'

Miss Barbellion felt herself persecuted, and thought it was time for a spot of retaliation.

'Holly, do you have any friends... over there?' she asked.

Holly did not answer immediately.

'Well, yes. Of course I do. I met some. But my old friends are still here. Like you, I mean.'

'Have you been to see any of your old friends since you – er – got back?'

'No,' said Holly. 'I do not think they would accept me so easily.'

'Indeed?' said Miss Barbellion.

She recrossed her feet neatly. The implications here needed consideration. Did this not mean that Holly was, so to speak, planning long-term residence?

'I see. So I am your only ghost-host, then?'

There was another silence.

'Are there many other – er – visitors – like you, say, in Bath?'

There was no response.

'I mean, when other ladies of my acquaintance practice their musical instruments do they, like me, have the benefit of round-the-clock supervision by young virtuosi?'

Holly refused to say anything.

'I only ask so that I understand the situation clearly.'

16.

After breakfast the following morning Miss Barbellion lowered the lid of her piano without playing a note and tiptoed out to the kitchen. Then she stopped. It was ridiculous, she thought, to be terrorised in her own private house by a wraith of no substance, a 'pianist' who had never got beyond Grade 4 (a very childish level), who needed to be taught her place rather firmly. Her own musical peace of mind had been disturbed by this impertinence, and let us remember, she told herself, walking up and down, that she had successfully played the piano in a hundred different places for a thousand different purposes and never mind if some of the notes didn't work or the whole thing was out of tune, did she ever complain? no, and she had made a lot of people happy in many parts of the world. Small, fat, hopeless ballet dancers by the roomful, fatally tone-deaf singers, shy boys and blushing girls, all needing hymns and folksongs and five million renditions of *Happy Birthday*...

Miss Barbellion boiled (slightly, of course, in ladylike fashion) with indignation.

She marched upstairs. She was definitely going to deal with this issue right now. She would leave a short, precise, clearly-written note about the difference between their respective musical careers, since as everybody knew, Miss Hocks was not given to gracing the premises with her presence in the clear light of a fresh, young day...

'Good morning, Nancy!' said a bright, familiar voice, the very minute she entered the room. 'How lovely to see you, again. I was just thinking how lucky we are, you and I.'

Miss Barbellion's fierce feelings began to subside. It was, admittedly, not really Holly's fault if she didn't know what the cycle of fifths was, and it could hardly be denied that her guest's conversation was never boring. Nevertheless...

'Lucky, you were saying?'

'Certainly. You have me, which must be great, as there is no-one else in this house for you to talk to, while for me it is important to be able to relax using the facilities here.'

'Oh, I see. How reassuring that is. That you can relax, Holly. And that our facilities are up to scratch.'

'Yes. I knew you'd be pleased.'

'Quite so. Oh, Holly, I meant to check with you, how good is your *sight-reading* at the piano?'

'Oh. Sight-reading.'

'Yes?'

'Actually sight-reading never came naturally to me. For Grade 4 you do have to do a bit. I just managed it.'

'Oh, indeed? You managed a "bit"? A few *bars*, in other words?'

'Yes. As far as I remember.'

'Uh-huh. I see. Not, for example, the whole of Handel's Messiah?'

'What is that?'

'The *Messiah*? A work of classic, global importance that has perhaps passed you by. Sung by a cast of thousands. With musical accompaniment. Usually a complete orchestra, but, in extreme circumstances, a *single piano*. Played at sight from the score, often at Christmas. With everybody depending on you. You get my point?'

She coughed, modestly.

'I allude to this achievement, one that I do not often bring to the fore, simply in order to put your passing of the Grade

4 London piano exam with its little *bit of sight-reading* into *context.*'

Miss Barbellion felt she had done enough to establish who was the superior pianist in the building. There was obviously nothing further to be said. She sat down.

'Yes, maybe Nancy, but I was only a girl, remember. And I was doing other things all the time when I could. Girl Guides. Playing tennis. Going to see films. Nobody ever asked me about handles. And maybe you did once play piano in the Olympics but that doesn't seem to mean that you can sail easily through that sonata now, does it?'

'Well, we shall see, Holly. And anyway my creative ambitions are different now. I have been asked to write a book.'

'That sounds like a more suitable activity for you. Could this be Cynthia's idea, by any chance?'

'In fact, no. Another friend. Elizabeth, as it happens.'

'Ah, Elizabeth. We haven't had the pleasure of her company here, as yet?'

'As yet we haven't. But she will certainly come to stay with me. She mentioned recently, by the way, that she doesn't feel comfortable with *children*. She hasn't had my experiences.'

'No doubt. Well, it will be interesting to see what she turns out to be like. Are you intending to write this book, Nancy?'

'Actually, Holly, no. I have no desire to do so. They want to foist it on me, but I am not going to play ball.'

'Why, is it about hockey or something?'

'It is about my professional experiences, all of which have taken place outside the British Isles.'

'I cannot see that leading to huge sales, Nancy. To be frank.'

'Well, you have no idea of what has happened to me in my life.'

'Possibly. But that is how it should be. Old people should be discouraged from reminiscence. That is what my father used to say and I understand why.'

'Well, if I do turn to literature I will not attempt to inflict selected readings on you. Given your youth and general education level and, I think it must be acknowledged, your attention span.'

'There seems to be a critical tone creeping in here, Nancy. I think there can be nothing wrong with my attention span. It was never singled out for remark in my school record.'

'Perhaps they were considerately sparing your feelings. This problem is not uncommon in young persons. In many ways it is not their fault.'

'What do you mean?'

'Well, an impatience with or uninterest in matters beyond their immediate, restricted world.'

'Can you give me an example?'

'Well most girls – I mean, well, flesh-and-blood schoolgirls – are only interested in obvious things; what might have happened in the past, here or in other continents, is irrelevant.'

'Sometimes, maybe. But perhaps whether things are interesting or not depends on who is doing the talking?'

Miss Barbellion laughed.

'OK, Holly, I have things to do. Think over what I have said. During your hours of free time. Perhaps something can be done...'

The doorbell rang far below, accompanied by a duet of urgent barking. Miss Barbellion skipped lightly down the staircase and opened the door to the postman. There was a large plump envelope addressed to her in Cynthia's unmistakable hand. She squeezed it. It didn't feel like garden bits and it didn't rattle. More like thick paper. It was an old shopkeeper's catalogue.

"Toys," it read on the battered paper cover. "BRITAINS LTD." Miss Barbellion opened it gingerly. Inside, laid out in separate sections in the most tempting fashion possible, were full details of all the lead toys of the Barbellion childhood, soldiers and armies, the farm series, the zoo series, the circus series and, what left her speechless, the gardening series. There were printed line-drawings of everything in brown ink, the prices neatly added in each case: a garden roller was a penny-halfpenny, the greenhouse one shilling and sevenpence halfpenny, and the most expensive boxed set seemed to be only fifteen shillings. The shopkeeper had pencilled notes of orders, and repaired the worn pages in the catalogue with adhesive strips from postage stamps, and it was the easiest thing to imagine the pleasure with which the deliveries must have been piled up under the counter and shown off under the glass. Now she knew the full extent of what was out there, all the different species of flowers, twopence a packet. There was even a pond with nymph and water lily. It seemed that the full lead range, undreamed of by toyshop parents and children, was not so far behind the plastic one, and there were other things that could perfectly well go in a garden, such as ducks, children on swings or bird tables, which were officially catalogued in the farm section. She groaned to herself and reached for the telephone.

'Mrs Dimmock, please?'

'Speaking. Hello, Miss Barbellion.'

' "*In introducing their latest series to the public, Britains Ltd, feel that they are filling a long-felt want, that of enabling the gardener, amateur or professional, to plan out his garden in a thoroughly practical manner from the laying of the beds, paths, crazy paving, arches, pergolas, etc., and last but not least, filling it with a large variety of plants in full flower and in nature's glorious colourings, arranging and re-arranging his design in miniature until a satisfactory one has been reached*".'

'Well, I suppose that is true. But there is no need to be pompous about it, is there?'

' "*On the other hand, regarded purely as a toy, Britains Miniature Gardening has no equal, as the novelty of making a garden, the beautiful colourings, the realistic appearance, will hold children of all ages in keen enjoyment for hours on end, and the interchangeability of all parts which compose Britains Miniature Gardening has been given very careful consideration by the designers so that even with a small collection of pieces, very satisfactory results are possible".'*

'Yes, Barb, of course. We are long agreed. I suppose the same thing applies to the plastic stuff, though, doesn't it?'

' *"Designs, which may be made up from the various pieces, are almost without limit and it is no exaggeration to say that whatever can be carried out in a full-size garden, can also be previously prepared in Britains Miniature Gardening, and simplicity being the keynote of the whole, there are no difficult parts to fit together, no messy glue, nothing that even the smallest child cannot carry out and very thoroughly enjoy".'*

'OK, OK, point taken. There is no need to labour this, Barb; I am as convinced as you. Enough already.'

' *"With a kiss of the sun for pardon,*
    And the song of the birds for mirth,
  One is nearer God's heart in a garden,
    Than anywhere else on earth." '

'What the blazes is wrong with you Barb? You sound like a travelling salesman after too much sugar.'

'I am saddened that good writing and poetry should leave you unmoved, Cynthia. The world of commerce has affected you adversely. I was sharing with you the unsurpassable inscription that precedes the garden section of the old catalogue that came in the post so upsettingly this morning.'

'Oh, I see. I didn't have time to look at it. I did think your answers were a little robotic and antiquated.'

'Well, you've done it now. I have documented here exactly what there is that you have to find. It is marvellous, Cynth. You have to make a gigantic effort, and we will tick off each bit with an old, chewed pencil once they arrive.'

'I was doing that anyway, without the report form at the end of the tunnel.'

Miss Barbellion laughed, and thought she would just have a peep at the zoo series, just out of curiosity...

17.

A day or two after the arrival of the catalogue Miss Barbellion woke feeling feverish and ill. She knew at once what the trouble was and what must be done. She struggled to the phone and groggily dialled the number.

'Liz?'

'Yes! Good morning. I have just been feeding the birds. They are so -'

'Liz, dear, I am rather under the weather. I think we will have to postpone.'

'Oh, no! You poor old thing. And I was so excited to be coming.'

'It's my old affliction. Will call in a day or two...'

The old affliction was malaria. Once you get it it is always there in your system, the Mission doctor had told her on the Indian border many years before. She long knew what to do: there were special tablets and you had to keep warm and drink plenty of liquid. It meant several days in bed, restless sleep and no pleasure in reading; there was always the reliable old radio.

The great plan had been that Lizzie would come for a few days and then Cynthia would arrive for the weekend and they would all go out to dinner or the theatre and enjoy themselves with energetic dedication. This exciting, if not historic, scheme had been giving Miss Barbellion anxiety on two points. Would Cynthia take to Elizabeth, and would young Holly stay out of sight?

On the early morning of the third day, as if to consolidate her fears, she awoke to find Holly standing by her bedroom window. It was the first time, as far as Miss Barbellion knew, that she had ventured away from the playroom, and although the curtains were drawn it was by no means night time any more.

'What's the matter with you, Nancy?'

'Oh, it's nothing much, I'm on the mend.'

'Looks like malaria to me. My uncle Oscar had it from the War.'

'You are perfectly right. It is malaria. It resurfaces from time to time, probably when one is worn down or stressed by events. I cannot imagine why it should have happened now, given my happy and carefree existence in this house as you will have witnessed. But I am nearly better.'

'You sure you don't want me to fetch a doctor?'

Miss Barbellion smiled at the thought.

'You are very kind, Holly, but I know how to cope with it.'

'I hope it's not infectious. Not that I can catch infectious diseases any more, of course. But who is looking after the dreadful dogs, Nancy?'

'My mastiffs are tough nuts. I have made sure they have enough to eat. And they probably pick up lost children or cats in the street if they are still peckish.'

'That's not funny, Nancy. And there was me coming down to see if you were all right. I knew you hadn't died yet, anyway.'

'Well that was a lovely thought. How are you, yourself?'

'Very tired. We rode for miles yesterday and the day before. I am letting the horse have a rest tomorrow. Are you eating properly and so on, Nancy? Old spinsters often don't take proper care of themselves. They find them after the winter, frozen in their rocking chairs by an empty grate, reading a three-month old newspaper.'

'So far I have avoided the fate that you describe so evocatively.'

'Yes, well, maybe. Your hair looks awful.'

'I was unaware that I would be entertaining so early, before I would have naturally attended to that matter. I am surprised, I must admit, to see you so far from your usual haunts.'

Your hair looks awful

'Well I am irritable. I was looking forward to a chat and you haven't been up once for three nights. I got lonely.'

Miss Barbellion looked thoughtful. That her playroom ghost no longer felt herself confined to the playroom made her doubly apprehensive about inviting unsuspecting friends to the house. What if she came down when other people were there? Or threw things about, or made obvious ghost noises?

'Perhaps, young Holly, we should have a chat about your plans.'

'What plans?'

'Well, about your not infrequent appearance here.'

'What about it?'

'Well you do seem to be here rather a good deal nowadays, rather than... well, anywhere else.'

'Are you thinking about rent, Nancy?'

'Not immediately. But I do have to think about the future. Next year I shall be seventy-three.'

'Do you think that is some kind of record?'

'It is for me. Although if you could read our family tree you would perceive that the women in this family tend to last a regrettably long time.'

'Of course I can read, Nancy. That was unworthy of you, if not mean. Although I haven't had much practice lately. I went to school like everybody else and had started well at my secondary school.'

'Well, if you are intending to stay I was thinking we could look at that. Some French and Spanish, perhaps. Regular classes with practice and pronunciation. And I am thinking of a little mathematics. We really shouldn't let those things slide, should we? We can work on your power of concentration, too. While you *are* here, I mean.'

There was no response at all to these suggestions.

'You see, I will soon be fighting fit as normal and I have a lot of experience of helping children on who are at a bit of a disadvantage...'

18.

Once reassured that there was no danger of contagious overseas fevers the good Cynthia did turn up for the weekend, but she went off a good deal during this visit on unspecified missions of her own around the city. The two ladies had therefore not spent so much time together in the top room, partly on purpose as far as Miss Barbellion was concerned, since she was still uneasy in her mind about what might happen with Holly. Cynthia did spend one session alone the day before trying to persuade herself that the new batch of furniture which she had got her hands on was of the right scale for the Barbellion doll's house, although it was immediately obvious to anyone who faced the situation directly – Miss Barbellion for example – that it was all too small. There had been no update on this sensitive issue.

'Listen Barb, I have an idea. Why don't you come back to Harrogate with me for a few days? There's room enough in the car for the odd defrocked missionary, and you can help me in the shop over the long weekend. What do you say?'

Miss Barbellion said yes without hesitation, and went at once to pack an over-weekend bag, selecting certain items appropriate for an assistant in an upmarket antique shop. Then she had to settle the dogs peacefully. This time they looked at her less reproachfully; evidently if she were going with Cynthia there was nothing to worry about.

When she nipped up to the playroom on her own just before they left she was surprised to find the doll's house furniture in a mess, with quite a lot on the floor and some of her garden display knocked over. This was hardly the work of Cynthia in a fit of pique and it wasn't hard to guess who might be responsible. There was no time to tidy up, though, and she ran downstairs to the waiting car, saying nothing, of course, of what she had seen.

Cynthia talked non-stop during the journey and drove with a disregard for convention that would have discomfited any passenger of weak mien. To stiffen herself Miss Barbellion thought back to lame donkeys on narrow mountain paths and sedan chairs over rope bridges, although she still closed her eyes when they approached any kind of roundabout. They went straight to the shop to offload certain packages from the back of the car. It was a tasteful premises, the exterior paintwork in black and the lettering (which partly commemorated Cynthia's second husband) in gold over the shop front and right across the central window. The stock was preponderantly smaller items, side tables, writing slopes, pretty lamps and chairs, and a great deal of sewing equipment in glass cabinets or under the counter. Cynthia shrugged at Miss Barbellion's unspoken enquiry, for she had been an unimpressive seamstress at their first shared school.

'People collect these things. Thimbles. Cotton reels. Cards of buttons. Many ladies come for them. I should have asked you about the Barbellion family sewing kit. I bet you have a smart thimble or two at headquarters?'

'I think there is a crochet-hook that belonged to Julius Caesar somewhere or other. What do I do about prices tomorrow? Do you indulge in that fatuous letter code to fox the public like A = 1, B = 2? I think that prices should be written on labels on things so people can see how much they are without asking, which is embarrassing.'

'That's what I do. I have labels so people can easily find out the price but I hardly ever come down. People always think that if you say £20.00 you will actually sell for £17.00

but I don't operate that way. Although if one of my regulars buys a number of items I usually bump it down a bit. But you needn't worry about that side of things. I will be here all the time and will deal with sales.'

The shop door clanged behind their first visitor...

'So, you have acquired a taste for the commercial then, Barb?'

Cynthia leaned out of the way as the waiter lit their candles, and frowned at the wine list, which was printed in small letters.

Miss Barbellion laughed. She had really enjoyed herself all day and been quite disappointed at 6 o'clock when Cynthia had swivelled the OPEN/CLOSED sign on the door and doubly turned all the locks.

'I love your blend of the gently sincere social worker with the ruthless graduate of Harvard Business School.'

'Well that is how I have had to be all my life.'

'Also, that gentleman to whom you sold the watercolour this morning was as much taken with you as with the landscape, in my opinion. Glad to see you've still got it, Barb; I shall have to keep an eye on you.'

Miss Barbellion lowered her eyes modestly but in the low light of the restaurant Cynthia did not notice.

'And what on earth did you say to that woman about the walking sticks?'

'I just said, perfectly truthfully, that I thought they were awfully cheap and that I had half a mind to buy them myself. I also said that this was my first afternoon and that I wasn't allowed by the owner to purchase anything in the shop. The lady nudged her husband and they bought all four.'

'I hope you didn't give them a discount.'

'No fear.'

'Actually, Barb, those sticks were priced rather high. I expected them to sit there for quite a while.'

'Well you'd better tell me all the bits you want to see the back of and I'll see what I can do.'

The next day they opened at noon. Miss Barbellion had been wearing virtually all the clothes she had brought with her since about 2.00 that morning, because Cynthia's house, some miles outside Harrogate and several sizes up from her own, had been the coldest building she thought she had ever set foot in. They had arrived late in a black drizzle of rain.

They had arrived late

The house was surrounded by gloomy trees, and absolutely full of old furniture. The kitchen was warm enough for them to sit and talk for hours, depleting the late Mr Dimmock's whisky holdings in lively collaboration, but the stairs were cold enough to silhouette breathing out or wheezing, and the bedroom, to which she was shown by her slightly giggly hostess, simply arctic. Washing so much as teeth was out of the question. Miss Barbellion crawled under the eiderdown in her second best overcoat and hoped for oblivion, thinking of summers in the Indian plains. She was amused on waking in the early light to see that the mantelpiece housed framed photographs of each of Cynthia's husbands, ranged in what was presumably chronological order, although Cynthia somehow managed to look identical in each.

The town was a-buzz with some kind of musical festival, and individuals in medieval dress holding trumpets or tambourines could be seen wandering listlessly up and down the high street. Shortly after they opened their doors an indistinct sort of person slid in and said he had "garden stuff" for the lady owner, a "whole bagful."

'Oh goody,' said Miss Barbellion. 'Can I see?'

The person bluntly upended the contents of his bag onto the glass counter. It was quite a large collection of old lead garden pieces, much of it defective and with most of the paint missing. Miss Barbellion turned some of it over with a fingertip. At last we've done it, she thought. Some proper lead gardens. Never mind the wear and tear. Good old Cynth. 'Hmmm,' she said out loud. There was a lovely example of the lead pond she had admired in the catalogue, and a nice little greenhouse. The person waited. He was sweating slightly in combination with a drippy nose and altogether far from prepossessing.

'Ten pounds,' said Miss Barbellion.

'You're joking,' said the person. 'Them's lead. Like she ordered. Got to be twenty-five to her. Bottom.'

'No,' said Miss Barbellion. 'This is virtually scrap metal. All the colour is gone. It's of no use to a collector. It would have to be completely restored for a connoisseur of any discernment and most don't want repainted items. Ten or nothing, and two pounds for your trouble.'

'Jeez-zuz,' said the person. 'Madame D. not in?'

'Not at the moment, I'm afraid. I'm in charge, now. I suggest you go and find some respectable-quality examples and bring them here. Then we can discuss money.'

'But they're Victorian,' persisted the unpleasant individual. 'You don't see stuff like that just like that.'

'Nonsense,' said Miss Barbellion. 'They date from between the wars. You could equally well claim that I am Victorian. I had a garden set like that. Still do. With all the paint still on.'

The man raised his hands in dull apology.

'And while you are about it, perhaps you could try and find us some miniature gardens in plastic too?'

'OK, OK, enough,' said the man. He sniffed.

Miss Barbellion opened the cash register and took out *twelve* pounds. She slid them slowly across the counter and looked across at him in her strictest fashion. The man pocketed the money, picked up his bag and departed.

Cynthia climbed to her feet with considerable difficulty. Throughout this exchange she had remained crouched on the ground behind the door to the storeroom at the back, searching in a bottom drawer for some unused price labels. She had recognised the runner immediately but stayed out of sight, hypnotised by her old friend's ruthless technique. She now leaned in relief on the counter where Miss Barbellion, with intense satisfaction, was setting out the lead garden pieces.

The pool was set off by part of a battered rockery, but the greenhouse was missing some crucial component and had to be propped up by the pencil jar near the register. In the early afternoon light the pieces made a most pleasing scene, and they were both happily fine-tuning it together when a well turned-out middle-aged lady came in through the door. She caught sight of the garden at once, pulled out her purse and said,

'Excellent. I'll be interested to take that group if I may. How much are you asking?'

'This is, I am afraid, not actually for sale. It has only just arrived in the shop and I already have a client.'

Miss Barbellion spoke up quickly. She started to gather her pieces together defensively.

'Oh, how absurd,' said the lady. 'Everyone knows I have been collecting these lead gardens for years and I've managed to procure nearly everything including certain factory prototypes, but I do need another pond with nymph. My pond with nymph is not all it should be, because my nymph just will not stand up reliably. I have had to make use of an artificial aid, which one doesn't like doing for lots of reasons.

eighty-five for everything

This nymph here seems quite stable, and although pale is interesting, and she will do me for the moment. But I will take it all while I am here. Some of it will be useful. Shall we say sixty-five pounds for the lot?'

She actually had her purse open, revealing an interesting thickness of currency notes. Cynthia said very firmly, 'I was thinking of eighty-five for everything' and stood deliberately on Miss Barbellion's right foot and pressed down hard. There was no way that the proprietress was going to watch an absolutely plum customer visibly laden down with real money leave her shop empty-handed. The desire to kick her assistant from Harrogate to the Himalayas was almost overpowering, but that perceptive individual, albeit with the greatest reluctance, remained silent.

The lady counted out the notes unhesitatingly and added her card.

'Do let me know if you run into any further pieces, won't you...'

She left the shop, swinging the bag from her forefinger with what seemed intolerable effrontery to Miss Barbellion.

'Cynth! How *could* you? I loved that pond. All of it. It would have been a real start on the lead problem.'

'You, Barb, are a very loose cannon, if I may say so. Seventy quid profit in two minutes flat is seventy beautiful quid. We'll get you better pieces, you just wait.'

People were coming in.

'Philistine!' hissed Miss Barbellion. 'We can discuss it afterwards.'

At ten to six she saw through the window the nondescript man who had come before, but he hung around near the door without saying anything, carrying a holdall. She waved.

'It's for her. She back?' he said briefly.

Cynthia judged that enough was enough, and came through from the back room, holding a sellotape dispenser as if very busy. The runner completely ignored Miss Barbellion and addressed himself pointedly to her boss.

'OK. I've been all over. This is a lot of stuff. But I am not talking about ten pound notes. Or *two pound bonuses*.'

'Would you like a cup of tea, Josh?' said Cynthia in a sympathetic tone.

'I would. I've been running everywhere all afternoon, since –'

'OK. Nancy, could you pop the kettle on please?'

She's getting me out of the way, thought Miss Barbellion.

'Surely,' she said, 'but do remember about condition, won't you.'

She disappeared through the curtained door as the man behind her blurted out 'Condition?' in such an aggrieved and bitter tone that she almost burst out laughing. She put in two sugars and stirred carefully and added two ginger biscuits to the saucer.

There was very interesting stuff spread out when she went back with the tea. A pile of old doll's house furniture, quite tasty, a few more lead garden pieces, part of a lead zoo set and a shop display box of plastic garden pieces. Quite a useful assembly. She poked at one or two, but Cynthia was already peeling notes off herself and it was clear that a satisfactory deal had been settled without her input.

'Keep looking for this stuff, Josh,' said Cynthia, encouragingly, 'and old Noah's Arks for the animals. I'll always be interested in what you turn up.'

'As long as it's you,' he said.

Cynthia followed him outside and stood talking to him for some minutes through the window of his car. Then it was all finished for the day.

'Listen, Barb, I have been dealing with old Leaky, and persons like him, for years. He is invaluable. I get some nutcase who wants fans, say. I nod in a thoughtful sort of way. I look into the distance as if recalling all the rare fans which might be in one of my storage boxes somewhere and I say, leave it with me, drop in in a week or so. They smile in appreciation and the minute they leave the premises I am on the phone to the right runner saying, get me fans, man, good, bad and repellent. They are my ambulance service, these runners. You cannot send them away with ten quid and two quid for their trouble. He was so offended that I could hardly get him to talk to me. I said you were my first husband's cousin and a bit of a film star and we had to treat you with kid gloves. I implied that you were practising for an upcoming role. He sort of nodded. I had to pay him well over the odds for the second lot.

'How much?'

'I am not going to tell you. All this garden and d.h. stuff is yours, of course. There is a bit of nice lead included. I quite like the zoo animals. Anyway, give me time and we will find a lead garden for you, I promise. Ponds, lakes, lawnmowers, everything in your old list. This furniture is cute, no? Look, he is a brilliant ferret, that guy, he knows where to go by some low instinct. He's heard of a dealer somewhere, for example, with a railway trunk full of old furniture for a mislaid doll's house that he is after for me.'

'O.K. Cynth. I shall try bravely to adjust. But that was a fine wee batch despite the paint loss... Anyway, I want to know what I owe you for this other stuff.'

'Never you mind. Consider it your wages. But I'll never forget your sending off that Joshua with two quid for his trouble.'

19.

'So there you are,' said Holly sardonically.

'Yes, hello, Holly dear. Did you miss me, then? I did come up to say that I would be away for a few days. I went to stay with Cynthia.'

'I simply cannot stand that fat Cynthia,' said Holly. 'Red faced and blowing like a steam engine. She has no business touching my things.'

'You're very uncharitable,' said Miss Barbellion. 'Anyway, she is much more interested in the house than the garden, and the house is mine, isn't it?'

'She certainly likes playing with my roller,' said Holly. 'Up and down the stripes of the lawns. She did it a lot when you weren't here. Whistling between her teeth. And the swingy seat thing. She likes to poke that. But she kept knocking things over. There are some of my flowers on the floor right now. I don't like her, Nancy.'

'Yes, I rather gathered that. I am a bit surprised that she knocked *all* those things over before without putting them to rights, though. Not like Cynthia at all.'

Holly said nothing. Miss Barbellion smiled to herself.

'And all that stupid talk about "the garden belongs to the house." You will have to put that right. My garden has nothing to do with that house.'

she certainly likes playing

'Yes, all right, Holly. You have enlarged on that already. You can't expect Cynthia to understand.'

'I want you to move my garden to the other end of the table,' said Holly.

'Cynthia didn't – er – *see* you, did she?'

'No. She would have apoplexy,' said Holly, 'and you would never be able to manoeuvre the carcass downstairs. I just watched and listened. She talks to herself. "Well, that's *that* done," or "We'll have to do something about *this*, won't we?"

It is so *irritating*. She will probably tread on the lead pieces if you ever get any more, or crush them with her bulbous elbow. And all that, "Ooh this is such *fun*, Barb," stuff. It is sickening. I was so glad when she left.'

'Holly, I find this clamorous outburst quite distressing. Cynthia is my friend, remember.'

"Possibly. All I can say is I am glad she didn't try to sit on my horse. I would have had to pull her hair and throw things at her.'

'Well, in my view it is not appropriate at all for you to be up here spying on me and my friends and cultivating such altogether unpleasant attitudes. Cynthia is in fact my oldest friend and in many ways a remarkable woman and I am sure that you can understand that for both of us there is pleasure in this whole thing. You have no right to take a stance like this in my house.'

'She is like a hippo with lipstick on and she has no right to touch my garden.'

'And another thing. Other people's conversation often sounds banal to an outside ear. Like a husband and wife talking in the seat behind you on a train. But words convey more than their literal meaning.'

'Well, anyway, I am not a spy,' said Holly. 'That was a very cruel thing to say. Especially given what has happened to me. If she comes back I am going to show her. I shall hide her stupid ironing board.'

'Holly, I don't want to have to be cross with you, but it is beginning to look as if it might be necessary. This is my home, remember, and my visitors are my affair. Your own status here is far from transparent. Well, I mean you yourself are in fact slightly transparent, but your attitudes are not.'

'Nancy, that is a very personal remark of an unpleasant type. I am not responsible for the way I look.'

'No more is Cynthia,' retorted Miss Barbellion. 'She has large bones and has, one can concede, filled out a little. All her family had large bones, as a matter of fact. But she has a true heart and her friendship has always been hugely important to me. She used to be a keen rider too, you know.'

'What, on a cart horse?'

'Holly, I intend to terminate this conversation. I suggest that if you find my friends and acquaintances intolerable you should hide in the chimney or somewhere comparable until they are gone. Most of the time you have the whole playroom to yourself, and there are not many girls who can say that, are there?'

'The next thing that you are going to say is "and finish your greens because of the starving children in Africa," isn't it?'

'That, too, is unworthy of you,' said Miss Barbellion. 'You do not know what you say. I have seen starving children in Africa. I am going downstairs now to attend to other things. I think it would be better if I do not see you here for a few days. And that you leave me in peace when my people come to see me.'

'I want you to move my garden away from that stupid house,' said Holly. 'You wouldn't like it if people interfered with your property.'

'Good night Holly,' replied Miss Barbellion, after a pause, and she closed the door decisively behind her.

20.

'Ah, Holly, we need to talk.'

It was a few days later. Miss Barbellion was quietly working at her table incorporating the fine new Harrogate bits of garden where they best fitted, and became aware that she had company.

'I am listening.'

'I have arranged that my great-niece Mina will come for another week at Christmas. When she breaks up from school. You are familiar with the fact that I have a great-niece?'

Holly made irritated noises behind her and gave the impression of being about to stamp her foot.

'We are still grumpy, then, Holly, or what?' asked Miss Barbellion.

'That niece. Your GREAT niece.'

'Mina? You know her, then? You were here when she came before?'

'Inky Pinky Mina, Mina the Moany Minor. The world's most boring person. Yes, I know her. The *artist*.'

'I didn't realise you were actually in residence then.'

Miss Barbellion suddenly felt and looked very thoughtful all over again. There was a long pause.

'We've been through this already, haven't we, Holly? My family is my family. Young Mina will undoubtedly be coming to stay here regularly as she grows older. And if we are thinking of very long term, I should say that it is not impossible that she might one day come to inherit this house herself.'

'You cannot mean that, Nancy?'

'Why ever not? I have no children of my own, and she is a perfectly direct sort of relative. We will see, but the possibility remains at the back of my mind. Mina is a lovely girl and very talented and not in any way at all boring. And, I think I would be right in saying, never *rude*. So, young Holly, I must ask you not to be so unpleasant.'

'How would you feel if someone moved in and took over all your favourite possessions? You wouldn't like it, would you? And, anyway, she already has a house of her own and a room of her own and things in it, doesn't she? Why must she keep coming here? She sits there for hours staring at my garden stuff and moving things about. And she is scared of horses.'

Miss Barbellion decided to ignore Holly and bent her head again over the table.

'What do you think would happen if *she* saw me? That would put an end to her little visits here, wouldn't it? She would run screaming down the staircase and out the front door and never come back, wouldn't she? I could see her safely onto her train. Ha ha.'

Miss Barbellion put down her planting tool and stood up. Her face was very serious indeed and she took a step nearer to her visitor.

'There are ways, young Holly, of driving you right out of this house, away from your horse and your garden for ever more. There are specialists who can do this. Bailiff sort of people. They come and do certain things and off you have to go. You know to what I refer?'

Holly nodded and looked at the floor.

'They are experts in removing unwanted 'tenants' and sending them back where they properly belong.'

She stopped speaking and looked at Holly, forlorn and penitent.

'I don't quite understand why you are here, of course,' she continued, 'since you have apparently never felt any need to tell me anything about it, but I am glad that you are come and I enjoy talking to you and I am happy you have access to your things. But it is one thing for me to see you and quite another for other people to have to. So I am telling you once and for all that you are strictly forbidden from any kind of appearance, contact, interference or other activity that might show anyone else in my house that you exist. In as much – if I may put it so bluntly – that you do exist. Let me be clear, Holly. Within this stipulation I include what you might call "accidents," such as a half-glimpse of part of you out of the corner of somebody's eye or some object having travelled from one place to another when it is incapable of independent movement. No funny business in a shady corner, of which we have several in this room, or provoking a half-idea in one of my visitors that there "might be something there." Do you understand me?'

Holly nodded.

'Also, while we're establishing ground rules it is equally important that you understand that you are confined – while in this building – to this playroom. I do not want you to start taking over the house and appearing in other rooms when I don't expect you. Provided you agree to these rules and keep them faithfully you may come here as you have been whenever you want. Furthermore, if you are a clever girl, and I am sure you are, you will find it in yourself to like my visitors. They are all interesting people and it is pointless to think of them with resentment. And, remember also, that this situation cannot go on forever. I won't go on forever, for one thing, although I suppose it is possible that you might.'

Holly shook her head violently.

'Well, you can tell me about that some other time. But just in case you are contemplating a regimen of regular manifestations under this roof, I will need to be able to feel sure that when the time comes for someone – let's say Mina

– to inherit the house, there will be *no ghost in the attic*. You follow me?'

Holly nodded.

'And do you agree?'

her head in her hands

She nodded again and turned her back on Miss Barbellion, sitting with her elbows on her knees and her head in her hands. Miss Barbellion felt more than a pang as she looked at her small, remorseful figure. But she knew that she was right. Mina in particular must be protected, in fact anybody who might come to the house. She had to be able to feel secure in her own mind. There was no more to be said now. It was a relief that a touch of the disciplinarian was effective with Holly; the last thing she wanted on her hands was a wilful, delinquent ghost of antisocial tendencies.

'Mina?'

Miss Barbellion spoke quietly, and Hilary, who had never heard her aunt on the telephone, did not recognise her.

'She's upstairs at the minute. Would you like me to call her?'

There were distant feet-on-the-stairs noises, and then there she was.

'Mina, I have just discovered a new word that you absolutely need to know. I was reading one of Dickens' Christmas Stories and there it was on the page: *bissextile*. It means "Leap Year." It doesn't sound like it, but it does.'

'Are you sure?'

'Well, I did have to check it in the dictionary. It means twice plus sixth; *bissextus* was the Latin name for the extra day we were talking about; Dickens certainly knew what it meant, and says that someone could have been called Bissextile if he was born in a Leap Year. I mention it to you so that you can incorporate it casually in a piece of homework. I imagine you have got lots of homework?'

'Heaps. It's not fair. Every time I finish one bit two more arrive.'

Miss Barbellion smiled to herself.

'Felix never used to do any homework most of the time and no one ever said anything. I'm supposed to work twice as hard now that he's joined the army.'

'He has really gone off, then?'

'Dad tells everyone he's joined the Foreign Legion. In France that's more respectable. But he is still unbelievably cross about it. He's put all Felix's toy soldiers in a box in the cellar saying they must have been a bad influence.'

'You don't plan to join the armed forces too, then?'

'Actually I did tell Mum I was interested in a career in the Royal Navy just to see what she would say. She went a kind of purple. I had to tell her twenty times that I didn't mean it.'

'What a cruel and unpleasant girl you are, Mina. I think it is a good thing your teachers give you piles of homework.'

Mina laughed. Then she paused.

'Is everything alright in the... house?'

'Of course it is, sweetie. Were you worried it had all fallen down?'

'Well you are all alone there with all those... dark rooms. I told Mum about it. She said it sounds more like a country mansion than a normal house. She thinks you need a suit of armour for the staircase.'

'Good idea. Better than a skeleton in the cupboard. Which I don't think we have, do we? I am fine here. I am used to solitude. Even in my playroom. And the dogs are always ready for a chat. But I will always be especially happy to have another Mina visit.'

'I had a lovely time. Auntie, have you found any more little flowers?'

'My Assistant Head Gardener is always on the lookout for something we can use. She found some plastic garden people, too, but I don't like them. They interrupt everything and look as if they are about to be noisy. The garden looks quite beautiful.'

'I can easily see it in my mind's eye.'

'If you ever thought about colours you could do a beautiful painting of it. I have an interesting question for you, Mina.'

'Yes, Auntie?'

'Say you did a detailed coloured picture of the garden with all of the flowers and the roller and everything, do you think anyone would be able to tell that it was not a real-life garden but a miniature, indoor one?'

'I've no idea. We would have to try an experiment.'

'OK, I'll get some paints in before you come next time. I wonder if I can still do it. You will have to teach me.'

'Did you paint when you were a girl?'

'A lot. Anyway, I need to ask you another important question about your Christmas present. It will be going under my tree, with your name on it in large letters. In due course. The question is whether you will be able to come and collect it in person after Christmas? Or will I have to harness the hounds to a cross-country sled?'

'Aunty I would love to come again. I'll ask Mum, but I will definitely have to be back for New Year's Eve because of Janet's party. I am going to wear the clinky necklace with the African stone beads.'

'Good idea. I think they have special powers. The man who sold them to me promised that they did. You'll have to tell me what happens.'

'When I come you must tell me all about what he said. And all your adventures. I want to hear everything.'

'That would take a hundred years. But we can certainly talk about some of them. And I have lots more funny treasures to show you.'

21.

'Are you there, Holly?'

Miss Barbellion had kept out of the way for two nights after their "discussion" but there was no sign of Holly now even though she had been upstairs for most of the evening. She called again softly, but there was no answer from the shadows, and she patted the waiting horse on the haunches so that it started a gentle backwards and forwards movement. Had she overdone it? Oh well, the girl will come back all in her good time, she thought, rocking the horse harder so that the creaking began, but the magic did not work and no rider came to talk to her.

There was no visitor the following evening either and Miss Barbellion became uneasy. She could not believe that Holly would really abandon her personal playroom facilities however offended she might be. Perhaps something had happened? But it was perfectly absurd to be worrying about a ghost's being out late on its own as if it were a teenager subject to maternal control. What could happen, after all? Car crashes, mugging or abduction could hardy affect such a creature, young and innocent though she might be. But a lingering anxiety persisted in her mind, and she found that she was listening for some indication that Holly had returned, the key-in-the-door sound that all parents wait for when it is very late, while supposedly occupied with other things.

Miss Barbellion was now finally removing some of Holly's unused flowers from their factory sprues. It was, if she were honest with herself, sad to be without her usual company of an evening, and she was just thinking that she would have to buy an extra radio for upstairs when there was a sudden "Boo!" behind her, and she jumped.

'I see you,' called Holly, and there she was. Miss Barbellion felt aggrieved.

'That is neither clever nor funny,' she said, turning round on her stool to face the grinning truant. 'Startling people is far from amusing.'

'Well I was just being invisible so I could watch you working.'

'I don't approve of that either. But I am glad you are back, Holly.'

'I see that you have decided to open my packets.'

'I wasn't sure about doing so, to tell the truth, and I was hoping to check with you, but we need some now.'

'Well I don't mind, Nancy. There is no point in keeping them like that, is there? I never had the chance to open them. At the end. I see we have acquired some altogether new garden pieces?'

'Yes. The excellent Mrs Dimmock has been on the hunt. Why don't you show me how you used to have your garden? Do you remember?'

'There was never enough space to set everything out together in our house. At least, the only possibility was the dining room table, and that could only be for a little while. My gran liked it when I was smaller when I had just a bit, but when she got old she stopped coming to our house and I used to do it on my own. When I was ill at first I used to make a garden on a tea tray but it was too easy to knock everything over. Your amazing table is perfect.'

'What was your favourite section?'

'Well, I always used to have a special flower bed with my special flowers in.'

'But there are lots and lots of flowers, far too many to have in one flower bed.'

'No, you don't understand. I mean my name ones. The *hollyhocks*. It went brilliantly in the middle.'

Miss Barbellion smiled. She had neither noticed the hollyhocks in particular nor picked up on their special significance.

'I say,' she said, 'I'm really impressed. There cannot be many girls who can garden themselves a name-tag can there?'

'Actually there was a girl in my class called Rose Plant,' said Holly. 'She could.'

Miss Barbellion laughed.

'There was a girl in my class once called Annette Curtain,' she said.

Holly giggled.

'Oh I know that joke. Did your teacher tell her to pull herself together?'

'It's not a joke, she really existed.'

'Yeah, yeah.'

Holly, meanwhile, was poking around among the supplies for more hollyhocks. There didn't seem to be any.

'My absolutely favourite idea was to have a whole row of beds of them, but my mum and dad always bought me something else for the garden. They didn't understand and thought I wanted one of everything that was available. And my uncle came round with a whole pile of garden pieces for me without a single example in it. I really just wanted lots and lots of hollyhocks.'

'Well we will have to see if we can't find some more. I shall ask old Cynthia to keep her eye open specially if you like. She seems to be a champion at finding garden things.'

'You would do that for me?'

'Yes, Holly, dear, I surely would. Cynthia is quite encouraging about our garden now. She just wrote to tell me she has found a whole bagful of pieces in very bad condition, few flowers left, broken fences, trees with missing branches and other bits that won't stand up on their own.'

'They must have belonged to some especially barbaric child who should never have been given a garden set in the first place.'

'I quite agree. But Cynthia wants me to make a new section that looks like there has been a heavy storm with everything damaged. She says it would be more *realistic*.'

'Really! Some people just have no idea about gardens, do they?'

a heavy storm

22.

'Barb!' called Cynthia awkwardly through the letterbox. She leaned again on the doorbell but nothing happened. There was a breathy snuffling when she painfully opened the flap again; one of the guardians was on duty in the hall and obviously keeping an eye on things, but it didn't bark.

'Listen, hound, it's me! Go get your mistress. Whisht! Fetch... er – Nancy. Good boy. I get Nancy, you get chocolate biscuits. Damn it, dog, it's cold out here.'

There was no response because Miss Barbellion happened to be in her garden, warmly wrapped up, trying to read her Sunday newspaper with a rapidly cooling coffee. Dog number two was by her feet. It was too blustery for convenience; the sheets would not lie on the garden table for two minutes together. She thought she might soon go back indoors. The dogs had obviously had enough bracing air already.

Cynthia meanwhile went and impulsively locked her car and prepared to wait. She had driven all the way to Bath, getting up at a wholly ungodly hour and leaving after the flimsiest of snacks. It was unlike Nancy to be out first thing on a Sunday morning. She sat down comfortably on the top step next to the milk bottles with her back against the Barbellion portal. It was peaceful and quite pleasant out of the wind. No need to go and look for a phone box. She would come eventually. Cynthia wriggled down into her large and heavy overcoat and before long she had dozed off.

After some time the door opened behind her. There was a joyful barking sound to be heard, triumphant and welcoming. Something enthusiastic was licking her face.

help me unload

'Hello, Cynthia,' said Miss Barbellion. 'How lovely that you are here. Would you care to come inside the house with the rest of us like you usually do?'

'If you help me unload the car.'

'After hot coffee. You look frozen, and I *am* frozen. Come in.'

'It is full, you'll notice. The car. With doll's houses.'

Miss Barbellion looked across at her friend's carelessly parked Renault. It was perfectly true. There was a tight jumble of numerous interlocked wooden small houses, which filled the whole of the seat area and whatever space there was in front. As for the boot, she couldn't yet tell.

'There are how many houses in there exactly?' she asked carefully as the door closed behind them.

'Er, twelve.'

Miss Barbellion knew she was not going to make it to the kitchen in one go. She sat down eloquently on the hall chair.

'Cynthia –' she began.

Cynthia held up her hand.

'Not a word at this stage. If we drink this promised coffee together are you going to help me unload the car or not?'

'They are moving in, then, your houses?'

'They are. You aren't meaning to suggest that there is insufficient storage space in this establishment?'

'Sufficient for all normal domestic requirements, yes, but not a whole model town would be my view.'

'Well, they are going upstairs on the table, next to your doll's house. The first, as it were.'

'They are, are they? I see.'

'They are a present, Barb. A gift. From me, for you. For your birthday. Well, your next birthday.'

Miss Barbellion smiled.

'Thoughtful. Or are you perhaps not rather accommodating your own birthday needs?'

'Yes, well, I thought we could share. Anyway, are you going to help me unload them or not? I have to park the car properly too.'

The two ladies went down the steps and Miss Barbellion waited patiently while her friend looked for the car keys.

'They aren't very heavy,' said Cynthia in a placating tone.

She unlocked the door to the front passenger seat and bent forwards. A modest sized doll's house with a cheerful red tiled roof and stencilled flowers on its creamy facade was then lifted out and placed carefully on the pavement. It was clearly a second-hand item.

'You could start with this. It is only a wee one.'

'Are there... things inside?' asked Miss Barbellion.

'No, I packed all those separately. There are two suitcases. You can't do any damage.'

'But they do have things?'

'Most of them have things. But we will have a lot of work to do to fill them up properly.'

'I can visualise that prospect,' said Miss Barbellion gravely. One would scarcely have imagined, she thought to herself as she carried the first prize up into the hall, that it was possible to get quite so many unwieldy objects into a single roadworthy motor car, but there again, Cynthia was a capable and determined woman. She put the wooden house down gently in the hall along the left wall so as to leave plenty of space for the other eleven. She stood back from it and smiled. It was very pretty and quite ridiculously small in comparison to what she thought of as the 'real' doll's house upstairs, but it was nevertheless endearing and she could easily understand Cynthia's enthusiasm, although there was going to be no necessity to admit the fact. She went back outside. There were three more houses on the pavement, neatly waiting parallel to the curb. One was huge in comparison with its neighbours. She stooped obligingly...

'That's the lot, Barb.'

'Surely not? Just these dozen? What held you back?'

'Barb, excuse my saying so in these forthright terms, but I am absolutely *starving*. I left before dawn. Last night, in fact. I now need breakfast, and by that term I mean sausages, eggs and, quite possibly, fried slice.'

'I follow you. I believe we can muster all those requirements. Leave your playthings here and we will see.'

'So you see, young Barb,' said Cynthia half-an-hour later, even though she had not quite finished her mouthful, 'Since I was last here I have come to a major decision. I am going to give up the shop, dispose of my stock at auction, sell the old house and buy a small flat with only my own furniture in it and things I like, and just, well, potter about. I think I can survive financially. I might do a bit of stuff now and again, but only if the fancy takes me.'

'I see,' said Miss Barbellion. She poured what remained of the tea and stood to refill the kettle. 'Are you quite sure this is wise, Cynth? Throwing over your life's work, I mean, in this giddy way?'

'Yes, definitely. Now you're back here, for one thing. And I shan't be getting married again. That's definite. It's exhausting, the antiques business. Financially unpredictable. Can't get proper weekend staff, as you know. And I have to have paid help nowadays to collect everything and move everything now Albert is no more. And he had started to grumble about it anyway.'

'Yes, I see. Have you already looked for a flat then? I hope you will have room for guests who want to get away from it all sometimes?'

'No, not yet. Since I saw you last I have been hunting exclusively for doll's houses.'

'Not without success.'

'That is nothing. Just you wait. But I thought I might have a look in one or two estate agents while I'm down.'

'Oh you are thinking of moving to Bath, then?'

'I thought I might. Depending substantially on your own reaction.'

'You anticipate that I might immediately move to Harrogate when I heard the news?'

'Sort of thing.'

'You weren't contemplating... that is... after all, Cynthia, as you have been the first to point out, this particular house is unusually spacious, well-equipped with bathrooms and always, I hope, welcoming.'

'Nice of you even to allude to the possibility. But I wouldn't inflict myself on you on a permanent basis, old Barb. It is good if we continue as we are, you here in the Palace, me in more of a local outhouse, so to speak.'

'And you would just use the premises here for stockpiling your new purchases. Pianos, billiard tables, recycled fridges...'

'Exactly. And when you wanted to get away from it all for the weekend you could come over and sleep in comfort at my place in the guest room.'

'Kind.'

'You wouldn't hate it then if we were neighbours in some measure? Not in a street like this, obviously. Some run-down bedsit, if that could be managed, suitable for a retiring person of my disposition.'

'Perhaps a prefabricated bungalow with no troublesome stairs?'

'That sort of thing. Mind you, if all goes to plan I should get rather a lot of dosh for the stuff. And old Albert's house and contents are worth a packet. Listen, Barbette, we have depleted a lot of your supplies and I shall be requiring a comparable breakfast again tomorrow, if not this evening. So, I shall pop out to the shops if I may. And when I get back we could stagger upstairs with some of the stately homes in the hall.'

'I think I will wait for your return before attempting anything.'

'But you won't be having at them resentfully with an axe in my absence?'

'I couldn't, Cynth. They are, at this brief acquaintance, rather fun. If one likes that sort of thing. Impoverished and post-Victorian in conception and manufacture, with something of the run-down bed-sit about them... provided, since they are so small, one can get them by the dozen.'

Cynthia laughed.

'Just you wait until you see them with all their bits of furniture in place. And the lights on. Then you will understand.'

The front door banged to behind her.

So they had both been approaching some form of crossroads, thought Miss Barbellion. The freshly-imparted news that she would be so close to Cynthia over the coming years gave her huge pleasure, and dispelled some unnamed anxiety that she had hardly previously registered. She knew that if her old friend were to move in permanently – even if allotted her own floor – it would not work out well long-term. And she had obviously reached the same conclusion herself. Had Cynthia really set her heart on moving in she would have said so outright, wouldn't she? Of course. And probably just moved in anyway. This new alternative would suit them both better. And Miss Barbellion didn't really, or at least not yet, want anybody else living there permanently. Guests, absolutely, especially Cynth, even for really long stays. But Cynthia abandoning her independent life and house and moving in full-time would require her to retract her own horizons substantially. She would no longer be able to sit unquestioned in silent contemplation on the stairs, say, whatever the time. Not that she was exactly prone to run about the house with no clothes on, but she always could. (If the dogs weren't looking.) This hot-off-the-press idea was the right conclusion, then. And they could be together as much and as often as they wanted. What fun ...

All this while Miss Barbellion was lying on the hall floor, peering through a whole range of small windows and testing front doors and garage doors for openability. Her favourite was definitely a smart stockbroker's sort of house from the 1930s, in mock-tudor style. It was capacious and had lovely windows and would be ideal to stock with appropriate "things." She was in the middle of a third sneeze when she heard Cynthia struggling at the front door. Her beloved friend was heavily laden with victual bags, and cakes, and there was a clink too, as of several bottles. They stood in the hall and giggled together, and Cynthia gave her a huge and long-lasting embrace.

23.

The theoretically fair division of labour was six doll's houses and one suitcase of furniture each, but two or three of the houses could not be carried by a single pair of hands. There were stops for the taking of refreshments, or sitting down en route without much warning, but in the end all twelve houses and the furniture supplies were up there and stacked on the floor. Both agreed, and it was roughly confirmed by Miss Barbellion's tape measure, that they could all find a place on the giant table, ranged round the edge, with the Barbellion house, the only building of any stature, of course, taking pride of place in the middle of the one long side with its back to the windows. The statuesque proportions of the latter made the new arrivals look absurdly small even when they were respectfully clustered, street-like, on either side. Miss Barbellion likened them unhelpfully to a "row of sheds." She further stipulated – and it was conceded – that the old lead garden as it developed would remain the private and exclusive territory of the Barbellion property, bolstered as soon as possible by pond and rockery facilities and shielded by lead stone walling and, particularly trees. Holly's extensive plastic holdings, already substantially augmented by various additions from Cynthia (with more promised), would be used for a magnificent back garden for the great house, from which the more imposing of the stunted neighbours might be allowed a certain share.

'Come on, old hippo'

All these innovatory steps implied a very great deal of work to come. Most of the existing garden installation would have to be moved and probably redone, while it was clear that redistributing the furniture resources among the other houses would highlight how much larger-scale treasure had still to be found to bring the Barbellion house back to its original splendour. She hoped devoutly that Cynthia had kept a record of what went in which house. She had, of course.

Although it was now getting late Miss Barbellion had got her second wind. It was exciting to have so much delightful work to do, and she was humming happily as she shifted houses and lawns experimentally here and there until she became aware that Cynthia was no longer responding to her remarks, but had fallen asleep with her mouth open in her preferred armchair. Poor Cynthia, she thought, all that physical exercise, and was about to tap her old friend on the shoulder and send her down to bed when she saw Holly standing behind the chair. She was laughing.

'Go away, Holly.'

Holly put her finger to her lips and disappeared into the gloom. Evidently she had consented to be a good girl. The sooner Cynth was tucked up in bed out of reach, however, the safer Miss Barbellion would be. Holly's merciless remarks came into her mind and, despite herself, she started to giggle.

'Come on, old hippo,' she whispered. But it took more than that to wake her up and get her to go downstairs to bed.

'What on *earth* is going on here, Nancy?' said Holly later, when they were definitely alone.

'To what do you refer?'

'All these hundreds of stupid doll's houses. And the garden in chaos. Have you both gone mad?'

'Doll's houses? Oh, yes. Those. They are nothing to do with me, Holly. Cynthia got them. She felt that the table here had a sort of unfulfilled potential. But she did pick up quite a lot of new garden things for us, too.'

'Are there any of my special plants?'

'Let's have a look. I haven't had a chance to ask her specially. Actually a lot of this bag is in rather poor condition. We will have to train her better. This looks like it was a hollyhock once, doesn't it?'

Holly smiled sadly.

"Now it's a ghost of a hollyhock.'

Miss Barbellion rummaged further but the plants seemed to be other types.

'I never really liked doll's houses,' said Holly. 'My friends all had one, more like these ones, but I never found them interesting.'

'Why was that, do you think?'

'I do not know. I think we can safely leave all that to Cynth and Meen, though, don't you, Nancy?'

'I think so. And to me. We all get pleasure from them.'

'I think I might be going away for a few days, Nancy.'

'Oh. Anywhere pleasant?'

'Nancy, it is time you understood that there are things that you are not allowed to ask me. I have told you that before, haven't I?'

'You have indicated something along those lines, I admit, which leads me, Holly, to certain conclusions, and one new point to share with you, if I may?'

'By all means.'

'Well, I feel that you permit yourself to ask me very direct and personal questions of a type generally shied away from among grown-ups, let us say.'

'To what are you referring?'

'Well, my age, marital status and history, how much money do I have. You have not yet asked me how much I weigh, or enquired about the regularity of my internal functions, but I am braced to deal with those questions too when the time comes. And there are broader enquiries that I anticipate: do I believe in God, reincarnation and so forth, although here I would inevitably defer to your greater experience.'

'That is not funny, Nancy.'

'I am not trying to be funny. I am merely explaining what I think.'

'Well I think the whole of that last speech was quite out of place. Anyone would naturally be curious about the person in whose house they are living. But with me it is different. It should be obvious to absolutely anyone that people in my position can say nothing about subjects like that.'

'I see, Holly. Well, like Cynthia I am a very tired person

now after all these exertions and must retire to sleep. As you will confirm I need about nine hours these days. It was different when I was younger. I remember once in East Africa –'

'Good night, Nancy.'

'I see,' said Miss Barbellion. 'Advance extracts from my proposed memoirs bore you. I bid you too, therefore, good night.'

24.

'Nancy, could you come over here please?'

Miss Barbellion had gone upstairs for a book to show Cynthia, which she thought might be in the children's bookcase.

'Good morning, Holly. What a pleasure to run into you while the birds are singing.'

'What is *this*?'

'Oh, that particular house is Cynthia's best find. It is called the *Princess Elizabeth*, apparently.'

'Are you going to float it in your bath?'

'How I behave in the bath is my own affair. When the Queen was a little girl she had a playhouse big enough to have parties in at Windsor Castle. This doll's house is a copy of it. Vintage 1932, apparently.'

'It is ugly beyond words.'

'This is scarcely patriotic of you, Holly.'

'It's too plump, the thatched roof is hideous, and it seems quite stupidly to open at the *back*.'

'True. It does.'

'Turned round like that, it is rude the way it sticks out its rear end. Anyway, it is not the design that is the problem.'

'Well, do share with me the fruits of your thinking, Holly.'

'What do you think that dust is, there?'

'Dust?'

'Yes. That dust. It is not grey, like all your other dust. It is brown. Like sawdust.'

'Yes, I see what you mean.'

'Do you know what it is?'

Miss Barbellion leaned over the table and poked carefully.

'Some old wood has rubbed off. Perhaps when we struggled upstairs with it. I'll fetch the dustpan and brush. It is impressive that you are so on the ball, Holly, if I may say so, with regard to domestic standards. Relatively few girls of your age -'

'I know what it is. It is *woodworm*, Nancy.'

'Woodworm? In this innocent doll's house? Surely you are mistaken, Holly.'

'I am perfectly right, Nancy. I know what I am talking about. We had woodworm at home a couple of years before I was ill. We had to replace all our ground floor floorboards. I am surprised that your famous tropical experiences have not prepared you better for recognising evidence of insect damage. Perhaps our resident *furniture expert* now in the kitchen will do better.'

'Actually, the green wood of the base is pretty flimsy here, and – oh my goodness, it caves right in. Oh dear. We'll never get a mortgage.'

'I think you will find that there are tell-tale holes throughout the house. Look at the chimney stack. The whole thing is probably riddled from roof to cellar. Serves it right. Pull up the carpets and have a look.'

Miss Barbellion opened the clasp and pulled apart the two wings of the back. Everything looked peaceful. She removed the dining furniture piece by piece from the back and —

'Forget that furniture, too, Nancy. The whole lot. It's also wood, isn't it?'

'Oh no, Holly!'

'In fact, having had a go at this one some woodworms are probably thinking now of moving up the table to try another house or two. There is not a moment to be lost, Nancy. I think, if you are very quiet, you might hear their little jaws going munch, munch. Some of them might relocate downstairs to your piano, you realise. Or they might eat the actual stairs. You would have to live up here with me.'

Miss Barbellion took no notice. Very gingerly she started to peel up the pale green lino that some previous owner had stuck down in the dining room. Underneath the wood surface was dotted with small holes and a light covering of the same tell-tale dust.

Miss Barbellion sat down on her stool.

'A thousand curses. You are right, Miss Hocks. But does it really spread so quickly?'

'Like lightning. You had better get that doll's house out of the house and into the garden as soon as possible. Douse it with petrol and *whoosh*. That's what my father did with our planks.'

'Holly, this is horrible. Dear Cynthia will be deeply despondent. I gather it was quite pricey.'

'This is no time for sentiment, Nancy. Think of your own vulnerable doll's house dangerously close. Go down and fetch dear Cynthia. I shall disappear. But I should be grateful myself if you would act promptly. I should not want anything to happen to my horse.'

'Are you completely pos, Barb? The Elizabeth one?'

Cynthia was wheezing rather badly, exertion being compounded by distress. She had been enjoying a leisurely breakfast with two newspapers and was a bit marmalady.

'Looks like it to me. Reminds me of carpenter ants in Borneo. Nibble, nibble. They always leave that tell-tale sawdust behind them, a million miniature saboteur-carpenters. I recognised the signs immediately. It will have to go right out of the house, Cynth. I am surprised that an old furniture hand like you didn't spot it a mile away.'

'Let's wait till we get up there. You might be imagining it. Anyway woodworm can be treated. You just have to spray it.'

They paused on the upper landing.

'My second husband had an antidote he made himself in his shed. I think it was supposed to be illegal hooch and the recipe completely backfired but it worked a treat on woodworm. Open the lid and they would run for their lives. The thing is that Princess job is a rare piece, Barb, and we have to -'

Cynthia lowered herself onto the stool and took out her magnifying glass. Behind her Miss Barbellion heard a noise like a snort of laughter. She spun round indignantly but Holly was nowhere to be seen.

'Damn this to hell!' said Cynthia. She looked around for something useful and then took a nail file out of her jacket pocket. She probed the roof and walls and various other places experimentally; there was nowhere the satisfactory resistance provided by healthy wood.

'Well it's a good thing you picked up on this, Barb. I don't think the other houses are likely to be at risk because they came from different places. This one has probably been left unloved in someone's garage. There has been no time since yesterday for it to spread. Even if they are young and athletic worms. But we'll check everything, of course. And the table. Using one's patented nail-file test one diagnoses in this case that the march of destruction has proceeded uninhibitedly over a long period. I fear that burial at sea is called for.'

'Holly recom—' Miss Barbellion began and then coughed very violently, struggling to extricate her handkerchief from her sleeve.

'What? You alright, Barb? Don't be upset. I'll turn up another cottage soon. What we will do is remove all the non-infected metal bits in case the next one comes without windows. And we'll need to spray the furniture, although it is rather horrible. You will have to give me a hand getting this safely downstairs again and out into the garden. We need to wrap it in a big plastic sheet and tie it up so we don't scatter worm eggs or whatever they use to reproduce themselves up and down the house.'

Miss Barbellion had recovered her composure and said she would go and fetch the winding sheet for the cadaver. Cynthia promptly set to work removing the windows. She certainly knew what to do. The metal window frames were held in place by little clips that could be bent back with the same nail-file. There was a depressing splintering noise behind her as she made her way downstairs.

'Confound it! There is a whole colony of something horrible under the roof here, Barb!'

Miss Barbellion grinned to herself.

'That was close, Nancy,' came a little whisper. 'Nearly gave the game away that time, didn't we?'

The clumsy great bundle swathed in black plastic eventually came to rest on the kitchen floor.

'Do we have any sausages left?' asked Cynthia.

'I think you are in the best position to report on that. I only had one and a half sausages myself this morning.'

'Hmm. The rest must have been pinched by the dogs. I was thinking we could cook the remainder over the conflagration.'

'That is rather insensitive, Cynthia. If not callous.'

'Come on old horse, the sooner the better.'

There was a rusty old dustbin at the back that had survived uncounted garden bonfires. The doll's house, shorn of its fittings and fixtures, looked pathetically vulnerable on the path as Cynthia bustled around for kindling. Miss Barbellion tried to imagine it as the pride and joy of some long-lost owner, but it was too blinded and war-torn to retain any vestiges of its former character. She shivered. Even on end, the house on its base would not fit into the bin. Cynthia came back from the shed with a heavy old garden implement of uncertain purpose, and began to cleave the miniature royal residence on the path with an accurate violence that rather startled Miss Barbellion, stuffing the dismembered corpse into the container. Soon the flames began licking up from beneath, smoke billowing through the windows and out of the front door in a horribly realistic fashion, and Miss Barbellion turned away knowing that it would recur, if not stopped at once, in horrible dreams to come. Cynthia, however, added the infected furniture like ingredients into a cauldron, and bent triumphantly over the glowing carcass, pounding the remains into a central glowing pile. She seemed inexplicably exhilarated by the annihilation of her expensive investment.

flames began licking up

'When it is cool we can scatter the ashes over the flowerbeds. The first outbreak of full-scale gardening since you arrived.'

25.

Cynthia, unaffected by the previous day's drama, went off the next morning to look for a flat much as if hunting for a new pair of shoes. Miss Barbellion strode off in the opposite direction with her dogs. She needed fresh air and exercise of a type unassociated with doll's houses and staircases or creepy worms and bonfires. They walked and ran and walked together and shared a large ice-cream cornet as a reward.

Cynthia was already home when she returned, much to her surprise, and in a state of high excitement.

'Barb. I have had an idea.'

'You surprise me.'

'It's those frankfurters. Or the brandy.'

'Possibly.'

'Yes, well. I thought I would go and find a small estate agent. I resent estate agents usually. Especially fat and rapacious ones. People should simply buy houses without them.'

'I have personally no experience of them. Inheriting Barbellion Towers, as you call it, made them superfluous. I do look in their windows once in a while, but merely to wonder what the people who work in them actually do.'

'Muse about how to spend their percentages. Well, I

found a highly uncompetitive establishment with unwashed windows and dead spiders and specialised grey house photos that have faded in the sunshine after months of unsuccessful exposure.'

'Were you hoping that their prices would be out of date like old stock in a bookshop, and get a bargain?'

'Perhaps subconsciously. Anyway, this drabbest of window displays gave me a brilliant idea. So I went straight in to find the manager. There was only one staff member on the premises, so that was not difficult.'

'No epaulettes or badges?'

'No, a modest and undecorated man in his early sixties. He is sweet. His name is Craigie. The hard-to-read painted letters over the shop front read CRAIGIE & CRAIGIE, HOUSE AGENTS AND AUCTIONEERS, so I hazarded that he might indeed be *a* Mr Craigie and got ten out of ten. Not the original one, of course. The Craigies are now perhaps commercially not what they were. The present incumbent, however, is by no means without charm.'

'How reassuring.'

'Yes, well, anyway I had this idea. Mr Craigie asked me how he could help, did I want to buy a home, and I said "Not exactly, allow me to explain."'

'Cynth, there is a lot of build-up to this story. Some detail could I think be bypassed, like when he said, "Please do," and you said, "Certainly," and he continued, "I have just the little villa that you need for your retirement, if that is indeed what you have in mind. Allow me to show our list of tempting properties...," or do I misjudge you both?'

'Hush while I tell you. What I said next was, "I think it would be a good idea to put an old doll's house in the middle of the window on the little display shelf where everyone could see it."'

There was a considerable period of silence.

'Cynth, dear. Sit down quietly now, there's a good girl. I know someone whose son-in-law is a psychiatrist at the hospital up the road and I am sure that with a case of this gravity I could get you a first appointment quickly...'

'Mr Craigie didn't say anything. Actually he looked at the telephone as if contemplating making a call.'

'Perhaps also to a psychiatrist.'

'Then he said, "Why would I want to do that?" So I said, "Please sit down and I will tell you." So he did. And I did.'

'Is that all we get for today's episode?'

'I then said, "Everybody loves doll's houses and I think that if you put one there everyone would stop and press their nose against the glass to have a good look." And Craigie said, "Why would that be desirable?" and I said "Well, it is important to make people look in your window isn't it and actually all shop windows or at least many of them in this country are really boring and unimaginative and are but seldom experimental or innovative and I have always thought so and in this case there is a special reason because what you would do would be to make a miniature FOR SALE sign exactly like the Craigie & Craigie ones you put up when you have a full-size house for sale and plant that next to the doll's house in the window as a magical advertisement and people would come in and then you could be charming about the window idea and sell lots of properties. As I assume you wish to do." And he just looked at me. So I said "I might be able to lend you one to try as an experiment, if you wanted." And then he said, "My sister used to have a wonderful doll's house. Years ago, that was. I wonder what became of it." He started staring into space and then he smiled at me and said, "You know that is rather a good idea. Why don't we give it a go?" And so I came home to ask you a couple of tricky and sensitive questions that now need addressing.'

'That doesn't sound like you at all, Cynthia. Usually a model of tact, with a sort of refined –'

'The main question is whether you might be prepared to lend one of your – as we know – long-treasured doll's houses upstairs for this purpose? If so, the second question is which of the surviving eleven would you be most prepared to relinquish? It means the awful task of selecting one.'

'It will be a wrench, as you indicate, and I will need moral support and wise counsel before passing the final verdict. But I already know which is my favourite and I have filled it with its own furniture. You can choose any one of the others, Cynth. Let us once more mount the great staircase together.'

So they did.

And the garden was there patiently waiting for her.

the garden was there

26.

'Oh, er – hello, might I possibly speak to Mrs Dimmock, do you think?'

The telephone seemed needlessly self-assertive to Miss Barbellion, and she had picked up with reluctance. She did not recognise the voice at all.

'Good morning. I am afraid that Mrs Dimmock is not here at the moment. She has been staying here, but this is not actually her house, and she has now left.'

'Oh, I see. Do you know when she will be returned?'

That was a funny thing. Cynthia had never given her number out before... but then it struck her that this must be something to do with the famous home-hunting scheme.

'Actually, I am not certain. But I can get in touch with her and pass on a message or a number if that would be helpful?'

'Yes, that would be most kind. My name is Marchmont Craigie. I run a local estate agents here.'

'Ah, yes; I know that she is looking for a flat in Bath. Have you managed to find something suitable for her, then, Mr Craigie?'

'Well, I am not actually calling about that at the moment, although we do have one or two possibilities on the books. It concerns, well –, her – doll's house.'

Cynthia's doll's house, was it now? So the truth was out

about what the invasion upstairs really reflected. Miss Barbellion smiled to herself after the complicated 'selection' process that she had recently undergone.

picked up with reluctance

'Oh, I comprehend,' she said sweetly. 'Her doll's house. What has happened? Does it need damp proofing?'

'Ho ho,' said Mr Craigie. 'No, an altogether different problem has presented itself.'

'Do go on.'

'Well, has she told you of her window-dressing scheme by any chance?'

'She did mention it, yes.'

'Well, it has boomeranged, rather.'

'Oh. I am sorry to hear that. In what way boomeranged, Mr Craigie?'

'Well, it's just that a lot of people want to purchase Mrs Dimmock's doll's house. They gaze at it through the glass, rush in full of excitement and want to buy it on the spot. They are not interested in our irresistible house-share schemes in Spain or recently-received generous offers or anything. They just want to buy the doll's house.'

'I see.'

'And they won't take no for an answer. When I say it is not for sale they say well it has a little sign up saying for sale doesn't it so it must be for sale and how much is it and can I give you a cheque? – all in one sentence.'

'Oh dear.'

'One or two individuals have offered really a rather large amount of money for it. I mean I was brought up to believe that property is a good investment and prices are always upwardly mobile but I didn't think that the same dogma applied to houses that are substantially less than two foot tall.'

'Well, it seems to me that anyone who concludes that an object in a high-street window marked FOR SALE is actually for sale can be forgiven for doing so.'

'Yes, that is what several individuals have argued rather forcibly. One said the whole thing was illegal; another indicated that his wife (who was with him and on the point of tears) was so disappointed that he would be consulting his solicitor about trading under false pretences and misleading advertising that very afternoon.'

'Goodness. Unexpected drama for you, then?'

'Utterly frightful. It is usually so peaceful on the premises.

So I was ringing to ask Mrs Dimmock to come and fetch it back as soon as possible. We really cannot go on like this. I would lift it myself from the window, but it is an awkward angle and I have done something to my back recently and –'

'Well, she lives near Harrogate, Mr Craigie. With the best will in the world I don't imagine she will be able to get back down to Bath for several days, and of course I can't answer for her on-going commitments then.'

'Oh dear, oh dear. Perhaps you, yourself...?'

'Well I would like to be helpful but I also know that Mrs Dimmock is very protective about her possessions and I don't think I would be able to cope with manoeuvring the doll's house safely out of the window myself if you don't think you could manage it. I wouldn't want the responsibility. She is very attached to that doll's house. I think she has prized it for a very long time.'

'Well this leaves me in a disastrous position.'

'Not necessarily. I have a suggestion.'

'Please share it me. I am apprehensive as we speak that another doll's house fanatic is going to burst in with a shotgun.'

'Calm yourself, Mr Craigie. My solution is of the simplest. You put up one of your boards when you are offering a property do you not? I rather think to have seen them when walking my hounds.'

'We do. They are individually hand-painted and regularly re-varnished. My father was very proud of them. It is very annoying when they blow down and get run over and so forth.'

'What do you do when you have effected a sale?'

'There is a white diagonal strip that we can nail on that says SOLD. The boy goes and does it. It is good for business, confirming that we do actually sell our properties.'

'Exactly. I propose that you make a miniature, to-scale white strip saying SOLD and pin it to the notice by the doll's house. Then you will be safe.'

'Magnificent! Wonderful! You are a *genius*, Mrs–'

'It is Miss. My name is Miss Barbellion.'

'Pardon me. Well, Miss Barbellion, I think you have hit the estate agent's nail plumb on the head. I shall go and paint one immediately.'

'Will you be able to reach the notice in the window in order to affix it?'

'I shall strive mightily. I am so grateful to you. I shall do it at once. Goodbye and thank you!'

27.

'So how much did they offer?' repeated Cynthia. She had interrupted Miss Barbellion's perfectly lucid account of her telephone conversation with Mr Craigie the moment that particular issue came up. Miss Barbellion made a shrugging sort of noise into the receiver.

'What do you mean you didn't ask?'

'Well why should I have? It is your doll's house after all, apparently. Its mere commercial value is scarcely my affair, is it?'

'But, Barb, this is crucial. If it is really a lot we should sell it immediately. I'll get you another one just like it. Find out...'

It was still raining when Miss Barbellion approached Craigie & Craigie's. She had her umbrella, of course, and was feeling light-hearted despite the disheartening drizzle. She stood on the opposite pavement under the butcher's awning. She saw what Cynthia meant about the hard-to-read writing over the shop. A cluster of rained-on people stood outside, but there was no overhead protection there and she saw that they all had their backs turned and were looking hard through the window. There were four or five adults and two girls. Miss Barbellion crossed the road in a desultory fashion as if uncertain which direction to take, and stopped behind them as if to check the property prices.

'Mum, can't we buy it? It's lovely. I love the windows. I want to open the front door and see who's there.'

'It says not for sale, poppet. Look at the little sign. Sᴏʟᴅ. It's just there for fun.'

'But it must be for sale if it's a shop. I always wanted a doll's house like that. Look at the flowers on the outside. Can't we go in and ask?'

The woman and her daughter went inside.

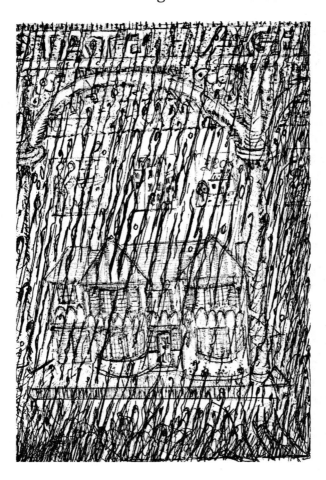

still raining

Another lady turned to her husband. She was ashen.

'God. I used to have a house just like that. I don't believe it. Now I look at it I can remember every single detail. I decorated it for hours with Rob and played with it every day, even when I was a teenager and had to make sure that none of my friends knew. It was always in my bedroom. My mother disposed of it when I went off to university. I was absolutely heartbroken. She just got rid of it. I couldn't believe it, and still can't really. It took me years to recover. It was really wicked of her.'

'I know, Steph. You told me about that when we first met. It was a dreadful thing to do. The same thing happened with my old train set. Went to some twerp cousin. Nobody asked me first. I always wanted to ring the NSPCC and complain. '

'But it's the same model, more or less. You know, I would love to find another one and do it up like my old one. Rob did all the tricky papering and the wiring for the lights. He was so patient and he liked it as much as I did I think. Can we see if they will part with it? It would give me so much pleasure to do that all over again...'

The little girl, however, was crying when they came out.

'Look, that one belongs to the gentleman, sweetie, and he needs it. It's a sort of advertisement for his firm. It's an old one, from like when I was a girl. We'll get you a doll's house for your birthday, how's that?'

'I want one just like that. Not a new one. It is lovely. I want to tell the story of all the people who lived in it.'

'I know. You could easily imagine all the little girls that it once belonged to...'

They wandered away, the little girl jumping disconsolately into the puddles.

The remaining huddle attracted other passers-by to peer round them to see what was so interesting and Miss Barbellion stood listening to what they said. No one, it seemed, could just walk past her doll's house or ignore it. And that, she thought, was rather interesting. Maybe Cynthia really was on to something with potential.

At that very moment, however, Miss Barbellion was suddenly overtaken by an enlightened but wholly uncommercial idea. She ran off in pursuit of Stephanie and her husband, scanning the pavement ahead: how would a husband offer solace to a deprived wife in the rain? There was a smart shoe shop in the next block. Maybe... Miss Barbellion stood in the doorway and shook out her umbrella. The place was crowded, people having discovered under the downpour that previously reliable shoes leaked. Then she spotted them, sat side by side like patients in a waiting room. Stephanie had untied her right shoe and was wriggling her stockinged foot. Miss Barbellion marched over to the row of little chairs and sat down next to her.

'Excuse me,' she said.

'Yes?' said the lady.

'I couldn't help hearing,' said Miss Barbellion, 'what you were saying about your doll's house and your brother.'

Stephanie looked at her in surprise, but there was never anything about Miss Barbellion's appearance to induce alarm and she smiled.

'He died, you see. And it was all his work, the decorating. It was my most precious possession. And she just got rid of it.'

'I understand,' said Miss Barbellion. 'Mothers can do strange things if left to their own devices.'

Stephanie laughed. The assistant came over with a box, and unwrapped the tissue paper. They were sensible shoes, but quite pretty: Miss Barbellion approved.

'Are you a novelist, Madam, may I ask?' said the man.

'I am not sure what I am right at the moment,' said Miss Barbellion with a grin.

Stephanie asked for the left shoe.

'Anyway,' said Miss Barbellion, 'I wanted to talk to you about that doll's house.'

They both looked at her.

'The one in the window, I mean,' she said. 'I want you both to have it.'

Stephanie smiled slightly, but shook her head.

'It belongs to me, you see. I've got lots. It is only there because of my friend Cynthia. But I can retrieve it the moment I want, you see. If you give me your phone number I will see what I can do...'

'You've done *what*?' said Cynthia.

'Well, it was important to them. We've got so many. I thought we could keep the sign and just put another one in. If you are still keen on pursuing this plan to do this.'

'You *gave* it to them?'

'I am going to. Tomorrow.'

'Even though Mr Craigie indicated that lots of people wanted to buy it?'

'Yes. Actually, we talked about that. He said to tell you that someone has offered him a hundred pounds for it.'

There was a very long silence.

'Barb, it cost me considerably under ten quid, that house. They're never very expensive. They're usually thirty or forty years old. Someone offered a hundred, and you are giving it away?'

'Yes. It seemed the right thing to do.'

'I am going into my kitchen in search of an outsize sherry. I will call you back. This is not what I expected of you, Nancy Rochester.'

'But I feel really happy about it, Cynth. They are going to collect it and take it home. Look, why don't you come back and stay and we'll have a d.h. pow-wow.'

'Wait while I knock this back. A hundred pounds you said?'

'I did.'

'Frankly I'm appalled.'

'You are over-reacting,' said Miss Barbellion. 'We have plenty of other doll's houses, remember. Mr Craigie said there was no problem; he is keeping the SOLD sign ready for the replacement. No harm has been done. In fact, he said he could take two, so that, if need be, he could sell one at a judicious moment – at a price to be decided by you – and keep the other there.'

Cynthia was suddenly uncharacteristically silent, but Miss Barbellion was absolutely certain from the other end of the line that she would have a gleam in her eye.

'Barb. I think you've hit on something. In fact, I have a whole new scheme unfolding here before me and, quite probably, a gleam in my eye.'

'I do wish you would make up your mind, Nancy,' said Holly, later that evening. 'It is like a railway station up here these days. All the coming and going. And all those stupid doll's houses. Upstairs and downstairs. One minute they are here, the next minute they are gone. I cannot understand why you should want them since you have such a big one already.'

'Yes, well it was not really my idea. And they are mostly gone now.'

'So we are back as we were?'

'I think we are. For the moment at least.'

'And dear Cynth?'

'De – Cynthia has found her flat. It is the other side of Bath. She is hoping to exchange contracts soon. And have a flat-warming.'

'Oh, goody.'

'I thought you would be pleased. It is an interesting premises.'

'Why is it interesting?'

'Well she has a little place over a workshop. It is an old industrial building. She is going to start a little business there, you see?'

'What business?'

'Well she has given up antiques. She is just going to sell old doll's houses. The plan is to find them and repair them and decorate them and then sell them.'

Holly said nothing.

I will always love my garden

'She will find old ones that are bashed up or falling to pieces and fix them up. Make them pretty. Unless they have woodworm, of course. Two of the students who helped me move in — before you arrived that was — are going to help her. One of them is a good carpenter, and it will be work for them if it takes off.'

'I hope you aren't rashly going into business, too, Nancy. At your age.'

'I think I'll go and help out. I quite fancy making curtains and things like that. It will be good fun. And repairing bits of furniture.'

'Don't you like your garden anymore?'

'I will always love my garden, Holly. You know that.'

28.

According to Cynthia, the Craigie & Craigie doll's house installation had engendered a direct knock-on effect on other window displays along the high street. She claimed as an example the boot-maker and shoe-repairer. She found out (by asking) that they had rescued from their basement an old working model of a small cobbler at his last that had not been seen by locals for twenty years or more. A wipe with a duster and a tweak of the terminals and the hammer of the little man rose and fell untiringly once again in the middle of their window, much to the fascination of all who passed by. Then there was the butcher. Seemingly out of the blue, he inserted in his own window a pre-war model of a cow whose meaty limbs and haunches were marked up in didactic fashion with the names of the various cuts. Not satisfied with that, however, he dug up from his children's long-abandoned old toy box certain farm hands – a milkmaid, a scarecrow and a man with dog and gun – and these were scattered admiringly round the feet of the giant cow as if exhibiting it for a competition. A week later and he had added a tractor pulling a wagon full of milk churns, and indeed no one knew what might be coming next. Cynthia's question was, and she put it forcibly, would those phenomena have taken place of their own accord?

a direct, knock-on effect

Miss Barbellion soon found that a deep scepticism on this point was a good way to rouse Cynthia to strong feelings, but it was she herself who noticed the miniature pug emerging from a lead kennel inscribed BEWARE OF THE DOG right in the middle of the pet shop window, surrounded by full-size kennels and other doggy paraphernalia, which (the manager told her, when she was in there for something or other) had led to the sale of several full-sized guard dogs within a week.

So, it was no surprise to either of them when the entire

window display of the high street toy shop shortly thereafter experienced an energetic face-lift, with an exclusive emphasis on doll's houses and their contents. Plastic, easy-to-assemble mansions paraded themselves under the lights, surrounded by examples of every item of furnishing or equipment that they had in stock. Come to us, they implied, to furnish your drab old doll's house in luxury.

Miss Barbellion made regular trips up and down the high street, enjoying the latest improvements, and was rather tickled that none of the establishments, least of all the garden centre, could apparently muster a display of old miniature garden materials, be it lead or plastic.

(There were other less respectable ripples, too; someone for a bet offered the local undertaker a small pickaxe and shovel and an old lead DEAD END road sign to install by the sample headstones in their window and was sent away with a flea in his ear.)

While this flare-up of competition gave much diversion to the immediately local population it did nothing to draw admirers away from the Craigie window. Many middle-aged ladies were moved to prompt action by the news that sometimes, when the sold sign was not in evidence, an old doll's house in that window could be directly purchased for money. This unexpected development became known far and wide, to the point that any given doll's house would usually go out of the door in exchange for ready currency immediately. It was Mr Craigie himself, learning fast from Cynthia's seasoned wisdom, who suggested that any incoming doll's house marked FOR SALE should go in the window at 12.30 on Saturday afternoon, from which point the establishment was totally closed until 10.00 on the following Monday, allowing the desire for possession to reach a fever pitch over the weekend among those fortunate enough to be in the market.

29.

'So, young Holly, do you think we might discuss your problem this evening?'

'My problem?'

'Well, you know, why you are... here. You alluded to it the other night, didn't you?

Silence.

'I mean to say, don't think me in any way intrusive, because it is lovely having you here, of course, but I was wondering, if you did have a problem, whether I might be able to help you with it.'

Silence.

'I am quite good at dealing with them, you see,' Miss Barbellion continued. 'I wouldn't wish to sound boastful, but I have had a lot of experience and –'

Holly sighed heavily.

'Oops,' said Miss Barbellion. 'Well, permit me to ask you one small, unobtrusive question?'

Holly nodded.

'Is your problem by any chance anything to do with the date of your... birthday?'

Miss Barbellion, having taken this long shot, was surprised at Holly's reaction. She jumped down from the saddle and came and sat down right next to Miss Barbellion on the window seat. Miss Barbellion had never been quite so close to Holly before, but she still did not permit herself to stare.

'YES,' said Holly. 'HOW DO YOU KNOW?'

'Well,' said Miss Barbellion, 'it is a bit of a long story. You were born on a rather funny date, weren't you?'

Holly nodded.

'I found out, in fact,' said Miss Barbellion, 'that you were born on February 29th, 1956. That is true, is it not?'

Holly nodded again.

'And I further established that your Tragic Death was also on February 29th, twelve years later. Also true?'

Holly nodded several times, and sighed.

'That means that you are a Double Leap Year girl, and it made me wonder whether that could be anything to do with your present trouble?'

Holly looked at her anxiously.

'It is,' she whispered. 'They can't cope with the paperwork. In L-i-m-b-o [she mouthed the letters] they just cannot cope with it. There's a whole load of people either born on 29/2 or died on 29/2 who have to hang around for ages waiting because no one is quite sure how old they are for the records. You can't get Clearance until they complete your forms. There are queues and queues at the windows and they always shut early. The worst cases are those who are Double Twenty-Niners, like me. The officer at my window always throws up his hands when I get there and says, "Don't ask me to work this out; I am not trained for this sort of thing, there is no precedent, there is nothing in the form to allow for it," that sort of thing. It's happened a thousand times. The same man. The same speech. Then I had a brilliant idea. I thought that maybe it might say on my Stone, you know how they do, like so-and-so born on such-and-such a date, died on such-and-such a date aged 99 (or whatever)? Well, I thought if my Stone did I could tell them and then they could enter that in my form. They would have to be satisfied if it was written in stone, wouldn't they?'

'That was a brainwave, Holly.'

'So I went to look. You can get out if you really want to, but you always have to go back for your papers in the end. But all it said was "In Loving Memory of our beloved daughter Holly Minchin Hocks, born February 29th 1956, taken from us to her Everlasting Rest, February 29th 1968." Not a word about how old I was. They probably didn't know, either. So I came back with nothing. And each time when I queued and finally got to the window it was the same clerk and the same thing, "Oh, what have we got here, that's a funny date for a birthday, we don't see many of those in this bureau, ha ha ha, look at this, ho ho ho." Then they read on and find the second date, "Well I'm jiggered look at this, what is this supposed to mean, must be some kind of joke, what odds would you get on that not that I'm a betting man ha ha ha." And it never goes beyond that. They have to fill in your exact age for the Evaluation. I used to hope that one day I would get a different clerk, but whatever line I stood in, sometimes for absolutely ages and ages, it was always him at the window, "Oh what have we got here etc. etc." And whenever I said please can you help me with my exact age it was always this, "Well, let's see, we have to fill in how old you are, right? So how can we answer that little problem? Normally, in cases of doubt, we double check by asking people how many PC birthdays (by which I mean birthdays when you get Presents and blow out Candles) they have had. That is our default system. Add them up and there you are: 1, 2, you know how it goes. All the way up. But you're not like other people are you? Oh, no. You only have one every four years, don't you? *Rara avis* I don't think. Well, if we count up your birthdays if you were born – as you claim – on February 29th 1956, your next PC birthday was on February 29th 1960, the one after February 29th 1964, the next February 29th 1968 when you died. That makes four PC birthdays. Any other kind of 'birthday' does not count. I have boxes on this form to tick for Ps received and Cs extinguished. Now, you don't look like any four-year old girl to me. Not a bit of it. And I must say that your whole case looks increasingly fishy the more I focus on it. I put you down as four and through you go at once because four-year olds don't carry Responsibilities, but where am I if someone checks? More than my job's worth. No one like you gets past my window, I can tell you. Next!" So once I found out the way back here I decided I just couldn't face that conversation one more time. And...'

always him at the window

Miss Barbellion listened to this lengthy declaration with the greatest attention. Bundles of different but related thoughts buzzed through her brain. Her first question was, what on earth am I doing actually talking to this troublesome phantom in my own house, and why am I not back in India? Then she thought, I can help this girl and probably no one else in this city possibly can. Then, after a slight delay, came another thought, rather sobering: Jiminy Cricket! If this has happened to her it could happen to me one day, a Twenty-Niner, and to Mina, another Twenty-Niner. And, eventually: the Barbellion dictum was to help in any way possible, and I understand perfectly the nature of petty-minded and vindictive clerks with a modicum of power behind an official window. Well, then.

'I can help you, Holly,' she said very positively. 'Cry no more, fret no further, ride your horse to your heart's content. I will help you.'

That Holly had those obnoxious dialogues off by heart was unbearably saddening. But, as she thought this way and that, Miss Barbellion gradually began to formulate what could be a highly effective and far-reaching plan. And if it all worked out as she hoped no one born on a February 29th would ever have trouble again. And as for those especially rare species who started and finished on one and the same date, they would come to be esteemed down there as National Treasures.

'Leave this to me.'

30.

Miss Barbellion's plan still seemed to her perfectly sound when she woke up the following morning, and that was a good sign. She would draw up a customised, official-sounding document sealed with red wax that would defeat the administration on its own terms. If it wasn't possible for Holly to take an actual piece of paper through (which didn't seem very likely), she would have to be coached in the wording so that she could recite it by heart in a suitably overbearing tone and browbeat her enemy completely. Miss Barbellion would draw it up in pen, and then type it out without any mistakes and seal it. Theoretically she knew that it should not exceed one page of foolscap in length because no official mind could concentrate on anything that went on longer than that, but as verbal delivery seemed the only option there was probably no need for such inhibiting brevity.

She unscrewed the cap of her fountain pen:

TO WHOM THIS MAY CONCERN

You, Exalted and Honoured Official, Guardian of a Window, responsible for Border Control and Entry Procedure, do you hereby know and concede that we the undersigned, representing the British Government's Department of Correct and Proper Record-Keeping, do constantly acknowledge Miss

Holly Minchin Hocks to be a fully-fledged, exactly twelve-year old girl, about the measure of whose age there can be no dispute allowed. The Chief Registrar of the Whole of the Commonwealth, Direct Descendant of the Chief Registrar of the Empire, hereby declares that at the time of her regretted decease, Miss Hicks was 12 (twelve) years old exactly. The official state reckoning is that the period from February 29ᵗʰ 1956 to February 29ᵗʰ 1968 be deemed precisely twelve calendar years according to the chronological system first invented by Julius 1ˢᵗ, Imperial Date-Maker (and ancestor of Queen Victoria) and faithfully followed by all true administrators ever afterwards. As the fruit of pure enquiry and by the various powers vested in us we establish the following three points:

1. For each year of her life, this same female, H. M. Hocks, received annual Birthday Presents; we here submit two illustrative samples:

> *Year Two: white leggings, two cardigans, a teddy bear, a plastic teething ring, a squeaky dolly, and a book token for £5.00*

> *Year Eleven: a very considerable quantity of miniature garden toys in plastic including trees, flowers, buildings, lawns, chairs and tables (and, seemingly, a bird-bath)*

2. For each year of her life this H. M. Hocks received candles in the successive issue of one, two, three, four, five, six, seven, eight, nine, ten, eleven and lastly twelve candles. The colours of these several waxen issues can be accurately documented for reference; we offer one example:

> *Year Seven: red, yellow, green, blue, pale blue, white and pink examples.*

All seventy-eight of these candles were blown out completely. In most cases a single exhalation is known to have sufficed.

3. Distribution of both Presents and Candles, tracked on a graph, is shown to correspond precisely to the crucial twelfth-part calendrical subdivisions of Holly Minchin Hocks' life, and consequently exhibits conformity to the well-known Fragonoff's Line of PC Exactitude.

Thus we the undersigned (whose seal is appended) hereby authorise the recipient of this our document to admit her without hindrance or let, having received a full set of Ticked Boxes and Boxed Ticks. In addition, should any future case of comparable bissextile complexity arise with Twenty-Niners or Double Twenty-Niners, we recommend that this scroll or account be regarded henceforth as an Official Precedent that will likewise allow all Officials to authorise their unimpeded passage by means of their Great Authority at those afore-mentioned Windows.

Signed and sealed this day:
Nancy Rochester Barbellion MBE, BA (Oxon), MA (Oxon), British Government Overseas Mediator with Difficult Registration Officers, Part-time Midwife Extraordinary, Acting Coroner (in certain emergencies) and Oxford-trained authority on Post-Mortem Paperwork and Passes, using ye ring paternale of the lamented Reverend Edward Chauncey Barbellion MA (Oxon), D. Litt. (London), sometime Rector of this Parish.

31.

'It looks really smart, Nancy,' said Holly. 'Did you really write it all just for me?'

'I certainly did.'

'And with that lovely seal and everything. But it won't work. I can't take it with me. It would sort of disappear, like rice paper on a macaroon.'

'That is what I anticipated. You are going to have to learn the whole thing, Holly girl, like a Hollywood actress with a new script. We can take our time, get it off by heart. Then you can deliver it with the requisite authority and your enemy will crumble before you and you will waltz through the barriers.'

'Do you really think I can, Nancy? I never really learned much by heart. Except the National Anthem.'

'Well, you could try singing that, too, if you wanted. Gives the right sort of impression. But let's see how you get on with the document. Shall we do a bit now? You know what *To Whom This May Concern* means?'

'It means the man at the window.'

'Exactly. That man who gives you all the trouble, or anyone like him. But we are being smart and polite, aren't we? He will soon see it means him. You must speak it clearly and firmly and look him in the eye, drawing breath as infrequently as possible so as not to disturb the flow.'

It was a long haul. Not for the first time Miss Barbellion thought dark things to herself about Holly's schooling; the girl had clearly never learned any two sentences by heart on any previous occasion, but they persevered together. Holly proved to have a talent for mimicry, so her teacher pronounced each sentence with the rolling persistence of a herald whom no one could interrupt, as would the master-of-ceremonies at an expensive society wedding.

draped over the backs of the chairs

In order to fix things securely Miss Barbellion brought Holly some pencils and paper. Each paragraph, written down and read out loud a hundred times, began to find a niche in Holly's untried memory, and Miss Barbellion was amused to encounter her on more than one occasion walking up and down learning her lines and checking them against her copy, as she remembered doing herself for schoolgirl plays in that very same room sixty years before.

Once Holly could get through the whole recital without stumbling Miss Barbellion decided that they would have to practice using a mock-up of the dreaded window, so that every detail could be prepared in advance. She pulled the two old armchairs into the centre of the room and arranged them back-to-back with a space in between where she placed one of her brother's wooden chests. Then a coloured shawl was draped over the backs of the chairs to make a roof. Miss Barbellion sat on the floor behind the chest which made a rudimentary desk and adopted a face of extreme boredom and uninterest.

'Next!' she called in a languid tone and making as if to stifle an incipient yawn.

32.

They had arranged a final confabulation very early the following morning, as Miss Barbellion was supposed to be going with Cynthia to an auction at Exeter.

'I feel nervous, Nancy.'

'Holly, my dear, you are a perfect candidate. You have done all the work and you will sail through. I have every confidence in you.'

'You sound like a school report.'

'Well that is true in a way, but it is a very good report. What time do you think you will be off? I mean, if I am to be providing sandwiches and an apple.'

'About tea-time, I think. It is usually less crowded then.'

'Ideal. Just be clear and firm. Probably they will let a whole outing of Twenty-Niners through by the time you have finished.'

Holly looked doubtful.

'Well, I will be out all day, as you know.'

'Yes, Nancy.'

'Back very late, probably.'

'Yes, I know.'

'So I have a suggestion. Before you go leave me some clear sign that we can agree on now. If it stays there, that will mean that you are safely through and haven't come back. But if we need to think of another plan and you are here again, remove it and I will know to expect you sometime. It is just a precaution. But I will need to know for sure.'

'Quite, Nancy. We don't want to be making you jump just when you thought you were finally alone, do we?'

'Precisely. I suggest the Mr Noah from the old Ark. We could stand him on the bookshelf behind your horse. If he is still there tonight I will know that you got through. If not, just put him back with Mrs Noah.'

I suggest the Mr Noah

'OK, Nancy.'

'Right you are. I must go, little Holly. Cynthia is picking me up on the dot at 7.15, which is in three minutes. Remember, then: if Noah is still here next to the pencil box, I will know you are safely home and we won't need to think of something else.'

'This feels more like my home now, Nancy Barbellion,' whispered Holly, and with one of her short little waves she was gone.

33.

'I didn't tell you, but there is a huge vintage lead garden in nauseatingly perfect condition in this auction,' said Cynthia, happily carefree in the driving seat. 'Virtually the whole catalogue, I should imagine. It's your ultimate Christmas present. I am after it for you but it couldn't be a surprise because I needed you to come and help me today anyway.'

Miss Barbellion smiled absently. She was only partly present in the car with Cynthia, mostly thinking of Holly. worrying on her own, probably convinced that she couldn't remember a word.

'There are several lots we're after. One really old doll's house with damp and maybe other complaints. Should be a snip. And several others. And you never know what else there might be at an auction. We can do the viewing and then have fortifying fish and chips over the road before battle commences at 2.00.'

Miss Barbellion nodded.

'We will soon have to invest in a lathe and all sorts of tools,' she continued. 'And there is another consideration. If we do this efficiently we are going to need a better outlet than I can provide from the workshop. If we let people in there they will walk around and look at everything and ask about special orders and knock over the turps. The beauty of Marchmont's set-up is that there is a good wait and no choice. But he wants us to take over his back room as a showroom, and eventually wind down his real business altogether and develop my idea commercially together. He even –'

'Yes, Cynthia?'

Cynthia, at the wheel, swerved slightly.

'Well, he even offered to rename the company and call it *Craigie & Dimmock, Specialist Agents for Smallholdings.*'

'Did he indeed?'

'He's much younger than me, of course. Nine years, in fact.'

'Indeed. Cynthia, I seem to remember –'

'Anyway I'm in no hurry. He pointed out the huge number of doll's-house-less visitors who motor through here with roomy boots to their vehicles. He has great confidence in the plan. We'll see what happens.'

It was poorly lit in the auction house and only a handful of dealers seemed to be there, picking non-committedly over the lots and making squiggly notes. The big old doll's house stuck out on one table; it was even older than her own, but was in sorry shape. Cynthia partly opened it with one finger and held her nose. There was a smell of life-size mould in the rooms, and the old wallpaper was peeling off miserably. Miss Barbellion considered it a doubtful sort of investment.

Her lead garden was waiting in one corner not far away. It was divided into two huge lots, nestling in large open boxes on old cotton wool, and was, as Cynthia had claimed, in virtually perfect condition. It seemed to include everything, all the parts, as if it had just been delivered from the factory to a popular toyshop: all the flowerbeds, walls and trellises one could want, glassine packets of colourful flowers by the heap, seats and greenhouses and some sets still in the boxes she remembered; in fact, the whole contents of her old, brown-printed catalogue. Everything seemed to have survived miraculously. Despite her persistent inner distraction Miss Barbellion eyed the collection with desperate longing. She bent over the table.

a lathe and all sorts of tools

Cynthia motioned her to follow.

'You must never look interested, Barb. Someone watching who knows nothing about the stuff will decide from your behaviour that the lot is worth having. But what a peach of a group. I have never seen the stuff in such wonderful shape. If a specialist dealer has got wind of it we are sunk.'

Miss Barbellion thought gloomily of the aggressive lady collector in Harrogate.

'Come and look at the furniture and forget about it. I've made a packet lately. This is my responsibility.'

Miss Barbellion managed some bread and butter over lunch, and one or two of Cynthia's chips to keep her company, but it was no time for eating.

As her garden lots approached towards the end of the sale her stomach actually began to hurt, and she sat looking dully at the floor as the auctioneer disposed of a sequence of Japanese dolls (a fiver), a rusty clockwork train set (bought in), then Cynthia's big doll's house (a snip) and three other doll's houses (three snips). And then,

'... an astonishing pair of lots, to be sold separately, vintage Britains lead garden toys from the 1920s or 1930s, the complete issue in mint condition as far as I could see (and I had a good look, they are beautiful); several original boxes... I have several bids here with me. Let us open the first lot... shall we say one hundred pounds...'

Miss Barbellion, metaphorically at least, put her hands over her ears. Cynthia had said nothing about possible prices for the garden. She would just leave it to her. She thought of little Holly repeating her lesson over and over; she might have reached the desk by now, it was already 3.45. Would that mad passport do the trick?

'... 130 pounds, 140...'

I am sure it will work, it will be all for the best; she couldn't really stay in the playroom forever, could she?

'... 310 pounds... all done at 360; sold at 360 pounds to the doll's house lady at the side, number...? Thank you, Madam; and now the companion lot – including pond with nymph, very choice – also some interest here...'

I think she will get through and Noah will still be there.

'... sold to the same lady, thank you Madam, going to the same good home...'

'Barb. BARB! Wake up! We *did* it. Come on, we need to adjust our fluid levels immediately.'

And Miss Barbellion found herself somehow hand-in-hand with Cynthia, being firmly led away.

a very small, round table

There was a hot, cramped tearoom downstairs in the basement. Many people needed serving at once. Cynth was exuberant; she had secured everything that she wanted for the business and pulled off the huge garden collection for considerably less than she had secretly been prepared to pay. Miss Barbellion, incredulous at her acquisition and worrying fretfully about Holly at the same time, was a little shaky. 'Sit down there,' said Cynthia, pointing, and joined the queue, soon deep in conversation with whomsoever was nearby.

Miss Barbellion found herself sitting at a very small, round table with two elderly people, bright and birdlike and clearly brother and sister. She became aware that they were talking about the lead garden and gradually realised that they must have been the sellers, come to see how well it had done.

'Excuse me,' she said, 'would you mind if I asked you something about the old lead garden? It is I who have purchased it.'

'Did you? How lovely! Well,' said the old lady, 'we had that garden sixty years ago when we were children. We had every single piece that was manufactured, you know. The whole output, and often more than one example.'

'That is amazing. But, if I may ask you, how is it that everything is in such wonderful condition? It looks as if it were all made yesterday.'

The old lady smiled.

'That is what everyone has been saying. There is a simple explanation. Douglas' – she indicated her brother – 'and I had a governess when we were young. On Sunday afternoons she would take out all the collection bit by bit from the cupboard and very carefully set everything up on the dining room table in front of us while we watched intently to make sure everything was properly done. All the flowerbeds and the flowers in their packets. When that was finished we were allowed to look at and walk round the whole garden display for half an hour. After that period had elapsed our governess would put everything back again, also intently watched by us. So that is why all the pieces are so perfect. Miss Sawley was always very careful and we were never allowed to touch any single item ourselves.'

'And did that not frustrate you, did you not want to play with them properly?'

'No,' said her brother. 'We had plenty of other playthings that we could throw around and which all got broken in the end. This was something different. It was more like a show, like watching a play that you knew well. We were always fascinated and happy.'

Cynthia came over with Nancy's tea half in the saucer. She herself was drinking a can of fizzy orange and was going upstairs to pay for everything. Miss Barbellion was to follow in ten minutes to help load the car safely.

Most unusually Miss Barbellion fell deep asleep on the drive back to Bath. When they pulled up at her house Cynthia found the house keys and carried the precious boxes of garden pieces inside and placed them on the kitchen table. Both hounds were asleep and hardly stirred. Some guard dogs, she thought. She went back for Miss Barbellion.

'OK, sister, everything is safe. You don't have to wait to Christmas to play with your present. I'll come over for a proper look tomorrow. Now I must put these new doll's houses to bed.'

And off she went.

Miss Barbellion sat upright at her table with a glass of water. What a day, she thought, and remembered her mother saying the same thing many times at the same table. Eventually she stood up and prepared to go upstairs. Her wonderful new garden of lead could wait until tomorrow. Now she needed to find out about Holly.

She switched on the lamp inside the playroom door. The horse was not creaking or moving and everything looked normal. With reluctant step she went over to the bookcase and did not know whether to be relieved or saddened that her Noah was still in place. By their agreement, therefore, Holly must have got over her great hurdle and found her way forward.

She looked around to see if there was a goodbye message of any kind. There was no letter or written paper to be seen, but she half-expected something beyond the long-to-be-cherished admission that Miss Barbellion, in coming to her rescue in such strange circumstances, had given her a temporary home.

Sadly she picked up the Noah with the intention of replacing him where he belonged only to discover that the roof of the Ark house was off, and all of the contents was missing.

'Here we go again,' she thought. 'What has that miscreant done with my menagerie?'

She looked around, and then spotted that the garage door on her no. 2 doll's house at the other end of the table was untidily ajar. She opened it carefully.

Her two lead rhinos were standing stolidly side by side in the garage, looking up at her reproachfully.

It was a tight squeeze.

Then she noticed the camels looking out through the upper bedroom Mock-Tudor windows.

She carefully opened the two sides of the little house and drew them apart.

Inside she found the entire twinned population of her Ark disporting themselves throughout the rooms, climbing the stairs, squatting on the furniture, thoroughly at home and looking, in other words, as if they owned the place.

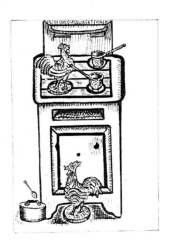

The gorillas and the elephants were even watching television.

Miss Barbellion burst out laughing and her heart lightened
and she blew a loud kiss in the direction of Holly's horse and
went happily to bed.

34.

For a day or two after these events Nancy Barbellion knew herself to be subdued and low. She was often to be found seated on the staircase with her chin in her hands but the dogs knew better and amused themselves elsewhere. Cynthia, who could easily have provided the right burst of energetic distraction, happened to be practically inaccessible. She felt restless in every room of her house, and had closed and locked the playroom door with symbolic resoluteness.

It was difficult to sort out what was churning around in her mind now her private ghost had departed. Triumph, perhaps, that her plan had defeated the monstrous border guards (and might even mean the rescue of other victims), but she shied away from that achievement and its implications. More complex were her own feelings for Holly and the reality of her former presence in the playroom. The only 'evidence' she could hold on to was the colonisation of doll's house no. 2 by the invading animals. She had thrown out Holly's original cardboard box that first afternoon. True, she had the papers from the Records Office, but they did not amount to much. Every time she looked at Holly's display it made her laugh. But what was to be done with it? Cynthia – and in due course Mina – if no-one else –would also burst out laughing when they saw it but assume she had done it herself, and would never accept it as the work of a ghost of whom they had previously heard no mention. But if she put all the animals back in their Ark her only tangible link with Holly would go. So it came to her with some sorrow that in the end she would probably not be able to hang onto a sense of reality about Holly and her problem. This unreality was inevitable, because the visits had taken place right under the noses of normal people in everyday Bath; she had ne'er uttered a syllable about anything to do with her ghost to man or dog. Had exactly the same Holly experience taken place in one of her old haunts outside of England it too would have receded, but into a sharply delineated memory to be recalled at will, like all her other memories.

Then, Miss Barbellion had a sensible idea. She would write down an account of what had happened, with all the details and all the dates, and include Holly's passport script. She would describe everything simply and directly, so that no-one later would say, "Well, she was in her seventies, you know, the sort of time when people start to get fanciful ideas. And she lived quite alone in that great old house, didn't she, and had never been married." But they would probably say the same sort of thing whatever she wrote about Holly, however matter-of-factly. It would depress Cynthia, who was much the same age and had been in the house much of the time and who would not know what to think, and it would sadden Mina, probably undermining their relationship for good when the paper came to light. Perhaps the sensible thing was to write out the account and include it among the Barbellion papers for the Society. They were accustomed to the testimony of English spinsters, and had no difficulty in trusting their statements and relying on their accounts. Many stranger stories than hers, at least in this instance, would be among their records.

Of course, she had her perfect new lead garden collection to look forward to, but she thought that an interlude from miniature gardening in the playroom above was called for and the huge parcel should wait till Christmas when Cynthia could plonk it under her tree and they could enjoy it together. Right now she had to get right away and make a change.

the ideal Christmas present

Perhaps this was the time to think about Lizzie's cruise? She would be able to rest the knee if it still needed it in a deckchair and drink round-the-clock concoctions brought by handsome pursers. In fact, they could probably find some bargain offer for two or three weeks until the middle of December. (It would play havoc with her practising, but she was beginning to think that her piano playing was already all it was ever going to be.) She would collect some tempting brochures and call Elizabeth; if she gave the go-ahead Nancy would make the arrangements at once.

While she was already wondering about warm islands and on-board wardrobe, the telephone rang: it was Cynthia, in noisy excitement. She had just picked up the ideal Christmas present for Mina.

It was a really tiny old doll's house that had only one room downstairs and one upstairs, quite a rarity to those in the know. Even Mina's bedroom at home could accommodate it, and it was a promise of bigger things to come. Cynthia clearly assumed that Mina would be spending her Christmas holiday being exploited in the Dimmock Emporium sweat-shop. And yes, what a *brilliant* idea to go on a cruise. With the famous Elizabeth? Wonderful. They should go on another one together somewhere exotic next year, all three of them. She had always wanted to, but none of her husbands had fancied the idea. Deck quoits and stuff. Of *course* she would take the dogs for a few weeks. A change of scene would do them good, and Cynthia had two more or less resident dog-walkers at her disposal.

Just before Miss Barbellion was to go off to the travel agent the next morning another huge padded envelope arrived in the post, this time from Mina. How wonderful, she thought with pleasure, she has really sent me a picture.

It was a bold, dark drawing of a young girl riding a horse. She was slim and upright in the saddle, a born horsewoman. The sheet was blackened with shadows, like all Mina's work. The backdrop field or racecourse was only hinted at, with the feel of the wind or the slipstream as they galloped together clearly brought out.

a bold, dark drawing

Nancy looked at it intently. She would treasure her own
Mina picture, and take it that afternoon to be framed. It
could hang in the playroom and remind her of her little ghost.
Miss Barbellion fancied, not for the first time, that, could
things have worked out that way, the two girls would have
been friends; she could imagine their conversation together
over the miniature gardens upstairs. She sighed, and turned
the picture over to see if anything was drawn on the back that
would mean a special sort of frame was necessary.

There was no second drawing, but on a label with a border of miniature flowers Mina had written in ink:

To
my dearest Great-Aunt Nancy,
from
her Great-Niece Mina.

There was something else inscribed below, too, in pencil.

Miss Barbellion looked up in astonishment and then with a private, wondering, lingering smile, for great-niece Mina had entitled her picture, in her most careful schoolgirl lettering,

Holly Hocks on the little horse.

ଜୟ ଜଗ

- The End -

CPSIA information can be obtained at www.ICGtesting.com
Printed in the USA
LVOW120051201212

312531LV00010B/321/P